SILK TETHER

SILK TETHER

A NOVEL

MINAL KHAN

YUCCA

Yucca Publishing books may be purchased in bulk at special discounts for sales promotion, corporate gifts, fund-raising, or educational purposes. Special editions can also be created to specifications. For details, contact the Special Sales Department, Yucca Publishing, 307 West 36th Street, 11th Floor, New York, NY 10018 or yucca@skyhorsepublishing.com.

Yucca Publishing® is an imprint of Skyhorse Publishing, Inc.®, a Delaware corporation.

Visit our website at www.yuccapub.com.

10 9 8 7 6 5 4 3 2 1

Library of Congress Cataloging-in-Publication Data is available on file.

Cover design by Kerry M. Ellis
Cover photo by Visun Khankasem

Print ISBN: 978-1-63158-070-3
Ebook ISBN: 978-1-63158-080-2

Printed in the United States of America

SILK TETHER

Prologue

"The TSA welcomes you to the United States." The plasma screen at the airport flashed at me sharply. A woman in a navy blue uniform grinned out from the screen. "Please have your immigration documents ready for the customs officer."

"Can I have your passport, miss?" The customs officer asked, hand outstretched.

I didn't need to look down to fumble in my bag. I had my documents ready in hand: college admissions' letter, driver's license, and after thumbing through what seemed like a mass of loose papers, all of uneven sizes, I found my passport with visa, nestled between two sheets, and offered it.

Why are my hands sweating?

I saw the officer look, *squinting* at the golden letters reading "Islamic Republic of Pakistan" for a while that seemed too long. I glanced at his nametag. TIMOTHY GOLDSTEIN. Timothy was a large man, his double chin deepening even further into his neck as he looked down at my visa. I saw him flip through every coarse page of my passport, flicking his eyes at the message on every page that notoriously read, "This passport is valid in every country except Israel."

Timothy was wearing glasses and his head was covered by a mass of thick, black hair. His eyes were heavy-lidded, tired; the look of someone who has seen thousands of passports and read indiscriminate words in dozens of languages. I guessed that he was in his late forties, perhaps even fifties. While continuing to flip through my passport he asked, "And what brings you to the United States?"

"I've been accepted into college."

"And which college is that?"

"Cornell University."

"Not a bad school." He looked up at me momentarily, in gruff acknowledgement. "And what's a girl going to Cornell majoring in?"

"Biology."

Timothy nodded and looked up at me. There was a long pause. I felt unsettled by his steady gaze, how his eyes darted across the points on my face, and then lingered at my hair, at my golden bangles.

"Don't feel uncomfortable if they look at you strangely," my mother had told me when I was departing the airport in Karachi, Pakistan. "They are only trying to figure you out."

The officer finally broke the silence and asked, rather abruptly, "What does your father do for a living?"

"He works in a bank." I responded.

"Are there any property or assets to your family's name?"

I once again searched through my stack of documents, and picked out a crackling paper listing my father's properties in Pakistan. The officer regarded my thin, creased paper closely.

"Are you traveling by yourself?"

"Yes." I responded. *Yes.* This became the first lie that I would to tell the immigration officers. My palms became moist. The manila folder I was carrying in my hands suddenly felt a lot weightier.

Timothy then asked me to look into a tiny, globe-shaped camera and press my thumbs down on the fingerprint scanner. I placed my index finger first. On the green plastic of the thumb scanner, I could see etched thumb prints of a previous person. I placed my finger squarely over the same spot, and felt the warmth of the fingers that had pressed down before me mere minutes ago. Thumb prints that were part of a ceaseless procedure; delivering data. Press. Hold. Release. Next.

I looked at Timothy, waiting for him to reach for a stamp. I then waited for the sound. That *crunch* of the stamp as it met with paper—*you are free to enter the United States now. Free to use our payphones, our dollar bills, hail taxis, mingle with our residents.* All because of a gray stamp on page three of my passport. My golden ticket. My ears were ringing and my heart was beating quickly against my chest. Thump-thump, thump-thump. *I am so close now.*

But I heard no crunch. Just the sound of typing. Timothy clicked away at his computer. He then reached out for a stamp and I watched him hover over my passport.

Stamp it. Go ahead! Just stamp it. I momentarily glanced to my right and saw baggage claim. A large, sprawling terminal filled with tumbling suitcases. People were hugging each other, rejoicing in making it home to New York City. I rubbed my sweating palms against my jeans and waited. *Please. Just. Let. Me. Go.*

But Timothy did not let me go. "Ms. Sattar." Timothy now laid down the stamp. His voice was stern. "Do you happen to know a Muhammad Khalid Sheikh?"

"Yes. That is my uncle's name."

"What does your uncle do?"

"He owns a travel agency."

"Is that right?" Timothy was not convinced.

"Yes, Timothy," I wanted to say. "In fact, "Muhammad Khalid" is a common name in Pakistan. More than that, the name "Muhammad" itself is an even more common name in the Muslim world, and in most Arab countries, it precedes the names of most men. It is the equivalent of 'John' or 'Steve' to the American world in terms of commonness."

I could say nothing, however. "Do *not*, under any circumstances, appear defensive to American customs officers." My father's words rang in my ears. "Remember, we are post-9/11 now. Everyone from our country is suspect. College education or no college education."

I now saw Timothy placing a yellow card in my passport. He handed the booklet back to me nonchalantly and said, "We need to verify some information. Please step into the room down this hallway to the right, marked X."

Room X. The room in the New York John F. Kennedy terminal that was dimly lit, discreet, harboring numerous cases that needed VERIFICATION. I walked in meekly and glanced around. The room contained a low ceiling. Fold-up steel chairs. There were several men of all ages sitting on the chairs; young boys; teenagers, and older men who were presumably in their fifties.

Only one unifying factor. All looked indiscriminately Middle Eastern.

I sat two seats away from a man with dark hair and the faint hint of a beard. He was fast asleep on the chair, his head tilted, head down. He snapped awake when he heard me sit and sniffed.

"How long have you been waiting here for?" I asked.

The man looked distracted for a second and then looked down at his watch. "Four hours." His accent was American, but with a faint hint of Urdu or Hindi—I couldn't tell which one.

"I'm sorry to hear that."

"I'm American, you know." The man looked at me, bemused. "Born in New Jersey. Visiting Pakistan for the first time. They told me in Karachi that as long as I shaved off my beard, I'd get past TSA no problem." The man chuckled and ran his fingers over at his scrubby chin. "Would've been a good time to listen to them. What's your story?"

"Pakistan-born. In Karachi."

"Oh yeah?" The man then said in mock sarcasm, raising his hands. "Well, welcome to America, land of the free." He then regarded me. "I'm sorry, if you don't mind me saying, you don't exactly fit the profile."

"Of what?"

"Of someone who needs *verification*." He used air quotes for the last word.

"I'm Pakistani and have an uncle named Mohammad Khalid Sheikh."

"Oh." He paused, thoughtful. "Sorry, that's just bad luck. Having a family member with the same name as the guy who orchestrated 9/11. Not a good deal."

An hour went by. And then two. Finally, after an additional half hour, a blue-uniformed man beckoned me to a thick brown counter, bearing my passport and documentation.

"We're going to need to look through all your luggage, Miss." Said the officer, looking pointedly at me, alert like a bloodhound. Then, as an afterthought, "It might take a while. But can we offer you something to drink, soda or water?" He held out his palms, a gesture of friendliness.

I looked at him blankly. He looked back, apologetic.

"How about some Starbucks?"

1

I was born in Karachi, Pakistan in the year 1989. The day the Berlin Wall finally came down. A celebratory time for many across the world. The end of an era. When the hands of the world jointly opened up in a disarming embrace to welcome the end of tyranny.

To reflect the celebratory occasion across the world, in 1989, a tradition began in my family: on every birthday of mine, my mom adorned me with flowers. "Why flowers?" you may ask. Two reasons. The first was because to my mother, the year I was born marked the *restoration* of Pakistan. The nation was recovering from a repressive ten-year dictatorship. Former President, Zia-ul-Haq, the leader who notoriously tried to "Arabize" Pakistan by introducing amputations for robbery and theft, stoning death for adultery, who banished liquor, cabarets, clubs and non-Islamic dress, had died in a mysterious plane crash a year earlier.

The second reason was a little more symbolic. 1989 marked a period of grooming for our hometown, Karachi. In 1989, the leader of a Pakistani political party—the Muttahida Qaumi Movement—launched a week-long Karachi Cleanup Campaign. More than 50,000 people heard his summons and worked endlessly day and night to leave the city sparkling. Rubbish and trash that had gathered over decades was cleared, and thousands of walls were re-painted. In a ceremony to mark the end of a spectacular and media-centered initiative involving the whole city, Altaf Hussein, the party's leader, showered MQM workers with rose petals.

Thus, the tradition of birthday roses was born. My mother has bought me a bouquet of twenty-two roses every year. It was now my seventeenth birthday. A big occasion for me. One that I wanted to mark ceremoniously, much like the rose petals that adorned my entry into this world. My mother decided it was good to go to a wedding.

My mother always said weddings were no laughing matter. "A wedding is the meeting of two souls; two families; two dynasties amalgamated into one."

So today I had agreed to come to my mother's cousin's step-daughter's son's wedding, which by the sounds of it was to be a huge affair. Ma had specially had a sari embroidered and stitched. We had visited our family tailor a week earlier to have the sari made, Ma clutching her royal blue sari in hand, and asked him to sow those few loose pieces of cloth into a regal sari gown, embroidered by the finest pearls.

Our tailor's shop was in the heart of the city's commercial area, known as Clifton. We had parked in a street noisy with the sound of motorcycles, the pavement dusty and cigarette-littered, and walked in to our tailor's shop with bags and bags of clothes. The shop was brightly lit. Fabrics in the brightest colors—magenta, orange, blue, scarlet red—hung from shelves that were stacked floor to ceiling, the popping colors belying the dank and dreary street outside.

Shabir, our tailor, walked up to us. Shabir was short, slight-limbed, but had extremely large hands, a trait I found somewhat extraordinary given his skill: tailoring. I looked at his thick fingers, trunk-like, and wondered how they could possibly find their way through a thread and needle. Shabir examined our fabric and casually made markings all over the dress. He didn't write measurements down, just muttered numbers underneath his breath and smiled up at my mother, "For you, madam, I will have this ready in a week," he said in Urdu, the native Pakistani language.

"*Bohot acha*," my mother responded, smiling. "Very good."

"Over my dead body he'll have it ready in a week." My mother turned to me over her shoulder, still smiling, and said in English, "One week means one month. Just watch." Shabir looked at us blankly for a second, and then went back to drawing measurements on the fabric.

Let me explain this blank look. In Pakistan, only a few spoke and understood English; those belonging to the upper class generally grasped the language, were privileged to read novels by Mark Twain and Charles Dickens in school, even discuss Shakespeare's soliloquies and write copious essays on modern American literature. For the overwhelming majority of the country however, English was completely inaccessible. Laborers like Shabir, though often skilled and adept in a craft, were barely literate. Indeed, a large calculator sat on Shabir's meager worktable, right by his measuring ruler and needles. Over the last ten years that I had been coming to Shabir's store, the calculator was always in the same place on his workstation. And ten years later, it looked brand new. As if it had surely never been touched.

When my mother turned to me and spoke discreetly in English, it was with the full comfort that Shabir could not understand.

"Next week means next week," she turned to Shabir and said in Urdu. Shabir laughed and responded, "Have I ever broken my word?" My mother bit back what was sure to be a sardonic response and left it at, "I'll be back again next week."

She then provided him with strict instructions to highlight the "twenty one pearls on each inch of border," and placed ten thousand rupees—the equivalent of a hundred dollars, on his work table.

And here we were, a mere week later. The sari gleamed a rich, dense blue color, with regal gold trimmings, in my mother's hands. Shabir had fulfilled his promise and surprised us all. And my mother got her requested border pearls, on every single inch of the fabric's border.

Ma was not a particularly great cook, nor the most dedicated gardener. But she was an aficionado of clothes. So I suppose it was a consolation that while the food may be lying burnt in the kitchen, and the weeds choking their last in the garden, Ma would, at least, have a gorgeous sari to turn to in her closet. Clothes, their intricacies and details, held an unflinching place in my mother's heart. Saris gave her the impetus to haggle with shopkeepers and to argue with my father. So you can imagine the horror that crept over my mother's face when I came out my room on the day of the wedding, dressed in a plain black-and-white *shalwaar kameez*, the Pakistani national costume consisting of loose, pajama-like trousers and a long tunic with slits running up the outside of the each thigh.

Nothing needed to be said. With a stifled sigh, I crept back into my room to change into something a little more dazzling. After many heated complaints (my mother's), whiny protests (mine), outright screaming (both of us) and tearful paranoia (my father), we decided on a maroon, silk-lined *lehenga choli*—a waist-length blouse combined with a long, pleated, and embroidered skirt, draped by a silky shawl that was tucked into the front waist. The blouse had light glass embroidery and was quite low-key for wedding standards, but for me, being the Tomboy that I was, it was just enough. Only when I appeared in this outfit before my mom was I allowed to cross the boundaries of my house for the wedding.

We left our neighborhood and drove through one of the busiest parts of town—Khy-bane Shamsheer. We passed auto rickshaws—three-wheel cabin cycles that were decorated with bright colors and are popular common 'taxis'—and passed motorcycles teeming with families, some carrying as many as five people on one seat: the determined man leading in the front, followed by three toddlers wedged between him and his wife at the very back, the children holding on to the bare limbs of each other for support. We laced our way through the crowded, car-humming, and winding streets to arrive at a spacious neighborhood, decked with houses that were large, looming, massive overtures of stone and marble nestling behind high walls. Each house had tall iron gates and boasted scores of armed security guards.

Outside the flower-draped wedding gates, two large men with AK-47 rifles stood to attention. I marveled at how similar the two guards looked. Both had deep-set, bloodshot eyes (from sleep-deprived nights?) and mustaches that curled just *perfectly* at the ends before turning upwards again. I imagined that both these men had stipulations in their contract with the security company. *Hooded eyes and upturned mustache required at all hours.* Or were they, in fact, close friends who liked to dress up the same, like schoolgirls who came to class, giggling and flaunting identical hair?

The two men looked straight ahead, unblinking. Their rifles jiggled momentarily in their arms as they nodded to us in acknowledgement. I wondered if those rifles were truly loaded, and what would really call for them being used at a wedding, of all events.

From somewhere distant I heard my mother muttering instructions to our chauffeur. I began to envision how these two armed men must spend their time while festivities were raging on behind those gates. Did they loiter about, to and fro, oblivious to the celebrations, keeping an eye out for the odd gate-crasher? Or did they take a peek every once in a while through those heavy iron bars, glimpsing at a world they knew they would never belong to because they belonged to the "laboring" working class? What did that feel like? Being a few feet away from a colorful world, a mere step, and yet being unable to cross an invisible line because of class? A line that no one on the other side would cross—the members of the "elite" class made sure of this because they were occupied in festivity and in wealth. United as a country, but divided always.

I was shaken out of my reverie by my mother's rasps. "Tie up your hair, it looks messy." Wasting no more time, we marched straight into the realm of vibrant colors, enticing music, and air-kisses.

⁓

"Ambreen, what a surprise! I can't remember the last time I set eyes on you!" And with that, the stranger leaned territorially in the direction of my mother's ear. The woman was tall and airy; something like what a model would look like two decades after her reign. Her bronze skin glowed against the glittery white of her sari. She delivered a hug to my mother and a kiss that drifted into the air. I waited patiently while the two exchanged pleasantries.

The lady then smiled in my direction. Her eyes shone like the sparkling diamonds on her neck. "And who do we have here?" My mother spared no time in introducing me. "This is my youngest, Ayla. You must have seen her before at Mini's wedding."

"Ah. So I did. Well, you look lovely."

I smiled back, and thanked her.

It was when Mira Aunty (the kind stranger) released my mother that I had a moment to absorb my surroundings. There were easily five hundred people at this wedding. These people were gathered in small clusters, little rings of women and men chatting intimately, touching each other's shoulders, reveling and talking about how "time had flown" and "wasn't it lovely to see families come together for weddings?"

A deep red carpet encompassed the entire venue, rolled out in one big scarlet wave. The yard we were in stretched out for 1,500 square yards, and neighbored a large house, which belonged to the hosts of the wedding. A bright yellow tent hovered over us and bore sparkling string lights. Lamps with lit candles shone brilliantly from every corner. Round tables teeming with roses and dandelions surrounded the yard; expensive silver china was already set out. The saffron smell of *biryani*—a traditional rice dish with spices, vegetables, and turmeric—filtered the air.

The food had yet to be served however. Everyone was standing around the tables, mingling and talking. There were young people: twelve-year-old boys wearing suits, and teenage girls awkwardly bunching up their *ghararas*—long skirts combined with a blouses—wondering how to handle all that extra material. We passed a group of older men in suits laughing loudly and patting each other on the backs while they easily held glasses of scotch.

A waiter dressed up in a tight bowtie and a too-loose large shirt approached me with a tray. "Martini, madam?"

My mother's eyes widened. "No thank you," she clipped before I could speak. Her gaze followed the waiter till he disappeared.

"Wedding hosts nowadays are so open about serving alcohol, it's disgraceful."

Selling liquor was indeed illegal in Pakistan. Under "Shariah" Islamic law, alcohol was forbidden. But that is not to say there was not a bustling black market in the trade. Sure enough, that waiter standing at the back of the large group of young twenty-something men in suits—the one snatching discreet looks here and there, was arranging shot glasses on a low-rise table, pouring a tall, regal bottle of Grey Goose vodka (most likely purchased in Dubai, a two-hour plane flight away in the United Arab Emirates, which freely sold alcohol, usually at a stupendous price) with the skill and experience of a seasoned bartender, assembling the little shot glasses on a large tray at seamless, lightning speed.

Consuming alcohol was definitely not the norm, however—black market or no black market. Social stigma surrounded sipping wine, beer, or any kind of liquor. Only a small minority in elite circles openly consumed alcohol at weddings and large social gatherings, places where one can disappear in a large, boisterous crowd of laughter and go by relatively unnoticed. Even then, my family—particular my mother and father—were not drinkers, and did not indulge when they were carelessly handed drinks at weddings. Personally, I didn't have a very big curiosity for alcohol. I did, however, enjoy observing people getting tipsy at these weddings. I liked seeing the way alcohol lowered social barriers. People talked easily, putting arms on each other's shoulders and leaning in to share jokes, becoming more intimate, more personal in a way they never would without alcohol. My mother and father's friends certainty lightened up a lot more when they had a drink in hand.

During research for a horticulture project, I came across a quote by Jeanne Olmo that felt so relevant when I came to weddings like these where alcohol flowed freely. It read, "At an award presentation for my father, Dr. H.P. Olmo, he commented that 'Maybe if everyone in the world would have a glass of wine a day, there might just be world peace!' As he was leaving the podium a man rushed up and said, 'But Dr. Olmo they don't drink wine in the Middle East!' Dad replied, 'My point exactly!'

I turned back to considering the wedding. Colors were carelessly strewn everywhere. Clusters of traditional yellow marigold flowers, scarlet rugs with silk *takiyahs*, or pillows, adorned the floor, alongside high round tables that held fine silver china, more flowers, and little pieces of *mithai*—sweet dessert for guests wrapped in fine ribbons and placed on every individual seat for each guest.

It was one big, glittering affair. Women's twenty-karat diamonds twinkled coquettishly when they caught the light, their saris fluttered, their expressions were airy and delighted, engrossed in conversation. The elder men bantered playfully with their business associate friends. The young men hung about in groups, casting furtive glances at girls they considered attractive. Everything was perfect. And unmoving.

I found myself sitting alone on the flower-encumbered chairs for most of the night. My mother was darting from one group of friends to another and my father was nowhere to be found. With no cell phone to entertain myself with, I felt bored. Perhaps even more bored than the bride, I felt, who was sitting on her throne, eyes lowered.

I considered the bride, slowly, as if I would never see her again, when in fact my life and hers would soon become intertwined in a way that would be startling. I would soon learn things about her later married life that would cause people at this wedding to gasp and spit out sips of their margaritas if they caught word of them. But of course, I did not know this at the time, as I sat there, sipping my Pepsi and appraising her.

The bride had caramel-colored skin, startlingly unblemished, and high cheekbones. Her lips were painted a deep crimson, matching the color of her *dupatta*—the head covering that draped her high, coiffured hair. Her wedding dress consisted of a scarlet red blouse, matched with a long, undulating skirt of red silk, embroidered heavily with the finest gold stones. Even underneath those voluminous layers of fine stones and fabric, she looked petite, almost frail. The gold necklace that sat on her collarbones looked cumbersome, too heavy for such a small frame. Copper-colored *henna* laced the girl's fingers, weaving patterns of flowers around the front and back of her palms all the way up to her forearms. Her expression was blank, neither happy, nor sad. She was talking to a well-wisher, her red lips busily miming words which I couldn't hear.

The bride suddenly changed her gaze and, with kohl-rimmed eyes, looked directly at me. Her face was artistically perfect, but expression-less. I sank back in my chair, taken aback, and tried to avert her gaze. Seconds later I glanced back in her direction. She was in animated conversation with an elder woman.

The groom sat next to her on a raised stage covered in rose petals; his traditional coat-like *sherwani* was crisp, and a flesh-colored turban sat primly atop his head. But that was where the pleasantness ended. His eyebrows met at the middle in a way that made him appear like a puffed-up bull. I looked at the bride, then back at him, then back again. She was a tender dandelion, he was a steaming bouncer. I shuddered to think how he would impose himself on her that night, his heavy bulk forcing itself on her tender flesh. Instinctually, I felt that this girl hadn't voluntarily landed into the arrangement.

My wandering mind was bursting with discomfort and pity. It was relief when the food was shortly served.

It was 1 a.m. by the time we finally left. My mom declared some of the guests were drunk as louts, and that we must leave before the drunker ones hurled profanities at us. The parents of the bride (the ones whom we were "related" to) were congratulated, and the hosts thanked. We finally made our way out of the gate. As soon as our feet crossed the porch, we were back in a crude and gloomy, but famil-iar, world. The colors of the interior were erased by the gray of the night. The boisterous aunties and uncles were replaced by ragged and sleepy-looking drivers.

I checked on the two armed guards that had stood like rocks at the gate and smiled satisfactorily. They had not moved an inch.

2

My alarm shrieked at exactly six o'clock.

I jolted awake, and banged it off. I was fortunate that it had woken me up this time. My previous alarm tunes had all been lilting and sweet. I had thought that it would be nice to wake up to the soothing sounds of my favorite Buddha Bar song. Wouldn't it be perfect, I had imagined, hearing the chirps of Indian summer at the crack of dawn? I suppose it would have if I had ever got around to waking up. The first few days the alarm had rung, I had not registered it. The soothing ocean sounds drifted away with the same ease at which they arrived; and they went by, unnoticed. Perhaps the sound of the waves had penetrated my half-conscious mind and beckoned me to sleep a little *longer*. Only after waking up late on two consecutive days did I realize the true treachery that Indian summer really possessed. I then changed my tune to a shrill, doomsday-trumpet holler. It was frightening enough to bring decaying fossils back to life. It also successfully managed to get me to school promptly at 7:30 a.m.

I stretched momentarily and blinked rapidly to adjust to the light. I ambled towards the bathroom and screwed open the tap. Cold water rushed out. I squeezed some liquid soap into my palm (mental note: I would need to get face wash soon) and rubbed it over my face, temporarily blinding myself.

Someone could creep up behind me and stab me in the back right now. Ok, in the next second. Or the next. Definitely after this very second. Someone is standing next to me, waiting to strike. I don't know it because my eyes are squeezed shut. I opened my eyes suddenly and glanced in the mirror, waiting to see a pale girl with a bloody, scarred face grimace back at me. The room was silent. I sighed. I never quite got over my fear of the girl in the *Exorcist*. I had watched the movie three times, hoping that the more I set my eyes on the fiendish girl, the more I would come to see her as just an ordinary person with makeup. But it didn't work. It's not as if she plagued my world, haunting me every second that I waked. But there were sporadic moments, every now and then, when I imagined her face as I lay down to sleep, and clutched the blanket around me a little tighter.

I quickly brushed my teeth and hurried out of the bathroom.

After I changed into my school uniform, I sat down to complete my Economics homework. I usually found myself completing work at the eleventh hour. Only at the last minute would my dormant conscience reactivate and give me a migraine, reminding me to complete laid-off homework, and study for imminent tests.

The sounds of the early morning *Fajr* prayer filtered into my room. It was before the crack of dawn that the *azaan*—the call to prayer—sounded most ethereal. The muezzin's voice acquired an intoxicated zeal that was unmatched at any other time of day. Ironically, it made me somewhat sad; I don't know whether it was my guilty conscience again, reminding me how much I needed to start praying, or the melodramatic hue of the call for prayer itself, that played its effect on me.

I finished my work hurriedly and grabbed my schoolbag; a dusty old black sack, and left for school.

⤙

I wouldn't say that my days spent at school were entirely mundane. True, the bell rang exactly at 7:30 every single morning, classes rolled before me on schedule, and every activity began and ceased at the whims of the bell. The system was rigid; timetables fixed. But the students made the school-going experience fluid. The school, without us, was just a gray block of rooms. We added zest to the inanimate halls and idle basketball courts, making it come to life the way Adam did when the Angel Gabriel breathed life into his dormant being.

On this particular day, however, things were a little more dramatic. I moved in a stupor from class to class, amazed at how little I knew about Napoleon's conquests. This wasn't just reflective pondering. I had a history test the next period. Funnily, I remembered the most interesting, yet academically useless trivia of Napoleon's life. I knew he was shockingly short for a political leader of such great stature. He hated the press, and banned some ninety newspapers from operating at the time. He delivered a heart-wrenching speech to his military men, thanking them for serving him loyally, right before he was sent into exile.

I entered the class in that same lost daze and sat in the seat in the furthest corner. My friends had already seated themselves before me. Alia shot a glance at me before the teacher handed the test papers out. Alia had been my best friend for eight years. It wasn't one of those kindergarten blood-sisters sort of burgeoning friendship that most people enjoyed boasting about. We didn't become friends immediately, either; it was much to the contrary.

Alia and I started off on hostile grounds. I vaguely remember my teacher introducing Alia—the new kid in class—on the first day of school of grade three, when I was eight years old. "Everyone, this is Alia. She is a new student here" My teacher pushed Alia, a skinny girl with a large head forward. Alia had thin, knobby knees and almost toppled over from the push. "Please make friends with Alia!"

My eyes widened when I heard the name, "Alia." *That sounds so much like my name*! I thought to myself. Ayla. Alia. This was terrible! There was no way this new girl with her big head was going to come to *my* class and just steal *my* name like that. Didn't she know there was already an Ayla in this class? Years later, we would have fun fooling our teachers with our almost identical names. We would laugh when we switched test books and wrote the same names on them, puzzling everyone. But at that time, in third grade, this Alia—this new girl— was my worst enemy.

After being introduced, Alia had come up to me on that first day of class in third grade. "Is someone sitting in this desk?" She asked, pointing to the desk in front of me. Her eyes were large and round, deer eyes. I narrowed my own eyes at her and said nothing, staring straight ahead, not making eye contact. But it was hard. Alia's head really was enormous, and she had a Beatles haircut. Her hair was boy-short and poker-straight at the time. She had a fringe that swept across much of her face. I was then, of course, devoid of any rudimentary fashion sense and had no clue she sported that "hairdo" straight out of her mother's *Vogue* issue.

But my eight-year-old mind pounced on her *boyishness* and let me see nothing more. I constantly snickered to her face, without knowing any better. Only a few months down the line could I realize just how much my juvenile gestures must have hurt her. She never responded to my cruel remarks; Alia was much too mature for that. She ingested my smirks and sniggers like a bitter pill; patiently. I suppose she felt sorry for me. Which is just as well. I felt sorry for the old me, too.

Then one day we were both stuck in school till the evening. Both of our parents had "forgotten" to pick us up and at a certain point we were the only two students left at school. 1 p.m. came and went, and by 4 p.m., we began talking, more to stop ourselves going mad than out of polite curiosity.

"Why don't our parents like us?" I asked Alia, swinging my legs vigorously on the school bench.

"I don't know. They may have really just forgotten to get us."

"Has your mom ever just forgotten you?"

"Yes, once in a crowded bazaar. I guess I just got lost."

"Lost? That's strange."

"Why?"

14

"I don't know. I would have spotted you anywhere with that hair." It came out sarcastic, unkind.

"Thanks. Even my dad tells me I remind him of Paul McCartney. Somehow he thinks it's a compliment."

That made me laugh. Then the ice not only broke, but melted away and evaporated into nothingness. We talked for two hours straight. About our families. Our parents' forgetfulness.

Eventually she asked me, "Have your parents ever grounded you?"

"No." I said.

"This feels like being grounded for eternity. Like this is worse than vengeance. Leaving someone in school till the evening. The school gatekeeper is looking at us like we're orphans." The burly security guard had come to check up on us twice. He phoned our parents for us. But nothing. Eventually, he bought us two ice cream cones to appease the abandoned children while they waited for absent parents.

At 8 p.m. I suggested, "Maybe they'll let us sleep over in the classroom."

"Nah, they can't let little kids sleep in a classroom," said Alia, "Eventually someone will call a cab."

"My mom says I should never step into a strange cab," I responded.

"Then you can stay here, while I hop into one and go home," Alia said quickly.

The thought of being alone made me frightened. It was getting dark and chilly. I could feel goosebumps under my school uniform. I realized grimly I'd never worn my school uniform for such a long stretch in one day. Had my parents really abandoned me?

Alia's father was the first to roll up. At 9 p.m. he swung by in a black car that looked polished like a dress shoe. He clasped Alia to his chest and sobbed. Actually sobbed. "Your mom told me she would get you from school. Four hours later I asked her and she said she thought *I* was picking you up. I'm so sorry! So, so sorry!"

Of course her father offered to give me a ride home. I accepted and we drove to my place, the polished-shoe car climbing through the narrow, tree-lit road that led to my house. I looked at Alia chatting freely with her dad about her day in the front seat. I couldn't help it. I was slightly disappointed that Alia and I couldn't spend more time together in that school. It was a lonely, scary four hours there. But I felt for the first time since I had come to that school that I had really opened up to someone. When I came back home and told my mom this, she smiled and hugged me, glad that I—the "loner" in the family—had finally made a friend.

And why hadn't my mom picked me up that day? It turns out she had indeed sent Nawaz—our good natured chauffeur—to pick me up. Nawaz had been working with our family for four years. He was a religious man. When he wasn't driving he was often sitting by himself under a tree in the front lawn of our house, reading prayer verses, or prostrating on his dainty prayer rug when the *azan*—the call to prayer—sounded. Nawaz was gentle, kind natured, but he was also absent-minded. And, as it turned out, he was not good in crisis situations.

On the way to school that day Nawaz crashed the car against the back of a truck, had an accident, panicked, and had escaped the scene. We found our battered Honda civic at the police station four days later. Nawaz was nowhere to be found. The only signs of him left were a pocket book of Quran verses in the driver's seat, and a set of prayer beads hanging by the rearview mirror.

In class that day, seven years later, Alia wasn't much different. Her hair had grown into long, undulating tresses, and she had grown very tall. At 5'7", she was taller than a number of the boys in our eleventh grade class. She was also classically pretty, with her large regal forehead and almond brown eyes. When she wore her thick rimmed glasses—before she got contacts—her face looked doe-eyed and whimsical. But her features belied an independent spirit. Boys went crazy for her because she fit this image of an accommodating, almost waif-like, pretty creature; something to be doted on, and sung to. But her humor was edgy and she was the most opinionated person I knew. The same doting boys would often leave a conversation with her, confused as to why they felt shunned, outdone.

Alia smiled at me from across the room, mouthed *good luck* and turned back towards the teacher. I would need more than good luck, I thought sadly. More like dollops, gallons, no, *oceans* of luck to get through this. My guilty conscience kick-started once more. It had had its morning coffee and was ready to get to work at my brain, effectively mincing it in half. I felt the onslaught of a migraine. My teacher laid the test sheet down before me. I flipped it over—I don't know why I even bothered—and read the questions. I read them again. And three times after that. Nothing registered.

Fifteen minutes had passed before I managed to put pen to paper. Another fifteen minutes trickled and I had only managed to write, "Napoleon Bonaparte began." I glanced at the teacher. She had sunk back in her chair, at ease, clearly enjoying her free period. She caught my gaze and raised her eyebrows in question. *Is something wrong? Yes,* I wanted to say. *I have a brain-block. Any remedies you may suggest?* I couldn't think of an appropriate expression that conveyed these thoughts. So I shook my head and looked back down at the paper.

I don't know what it was at that moment, but if I were seeing myself in a cartoon, a light bulb would appear neatly above my head. Crucial details started coming back to me. I began to scribble as soon as I remembered any relevant information. I even managed to squeeze in a conclusion before the bell rang. Just as I handed in my work, the bell trilled away, signaling us to get moving to our next classes. I groaned to myself. I had biology next.

My parents had always complained that my combination of subjects was odd. I could partly understand their concern. You wouldn't find too many people who took world history, biology, art and economics together. They were subjects from four completely different worlds, said my father. He had spent weeks trying to convince me to change my mind before I handed in my application. "It's like a vegetarian going to a restaurant and asking for some broccoli, a little piece of meat, a helping of fish, and a bit of chicken!" he had bleated. "You don't have the taste for technical subjects like biology and economics. Where do you plan to end up?" He had flailed his hands about helplessly.

But I persisted. I told my father some part of me felt it was good to be *well-rounded*. People can't really put much of a fight up against that word. *Well-rounded*. But really, the truth was—I had no idea what I wanted to do. I wasn't sure what I was even good at. With a blindfold on I aimed and picked subjects that sounded interesting, hoping to be led, steered toward some path like a willing sheep to a grazing land.

History made me feel introspective and I really liked how orderly mathematics was. And biology, well, biology was just a science I felt I should have. I had never been interested in learning names like *Lactobacillus* and *Glomerulus filtrate*. Nor did I look forward to dissecting a sheep's kidney. But growing up, some part of me had this yearning to learn a broad spectrum of things. I wanted to learn the intricacies of the ancient Mesopotamian civilization along with the workings of the heart muscle. I really did want to be multi-dimensional. If it meant working hard for biology, I would just have to do it.

After my first few lessons of Advanced Biology, however, I became bitterly disappointed. We didn't delve into the intricacies of the miracle that was the human body. We spent a month, instead, learning the chemical composition of plant sap. I became less intrigued by the day. I still studied steadily despite my lack of interest—I needed to secure those grades in order to prove to Dad that I was worthy of my unusual choice.

Over time, though, I began to perform my work and experiments mechanically. Flip. Read. Memorize. Insert. When we finally came round to studying the human heart, I found that it held less interest for others than it did for me. While my classmates were busy scribbling down notes on the right atrium, I was busy marveling at man's weakness. Even the strongest man was a weakling; so *reliant* on a fist-shaped pump in order to keep breathing. And how ignorant, too. Oblivious to the rhythm of the pulse that governs his existence. He neglects his heartbeat, abuses it. He slows its rhythm every time he gulps butter-soaked gravy. He increases its pace fiercely when he is stressed. He strains its walls when he is in love. And all the while, he is unaware of it, until the rhythm finally breaks forever and he is no more.

The different chambers of the right atrium, by comparison, held little meaning for me.

And, here was yet another biology class. There were more chemicals that needed identification, more conclusions to be drawn from what seemed like futile experiments. It was Tuesday, the assigned day for a practical. I almost cried as I lugged my heavy bag to the biology lab. Mixing solutions and heating them over a flame as part of the practical seemed easy. Just throw a batch of odd substances together and see what happens. Like cooking omelets. Simple. But it took a lot of time. It was a slow, droning process, aggravated by my clumsiness around instruments. This particular time my clumsiness proved disastrous.

Everything chugged along normally enough the first minute or so. I scanned the four test tubes in front of me, labeled K1, K2, K3 and K4. I screwed open the Bunsen burner. The tube hissed out gas at me. I struck a matchstick and carefully held it on top of the tube's mouth. *Voila!* It was burning. No one around me spoke a word. All I heard was the tinkle of the test tubes and the *hisss* of the Bunsen flame. Everyone was fixated on their work, trying desperately to unravel the mystery behind this phenomenon: the identity of K1.

"Check the temperature of the water constantly," my biology teacher instructed from the head of the room. She was tall and broad-shouldered, with thick-framed glasses resting on the top of her nose. I liked to speculate whether she was Amazonian. It certainly made biology more interesting for me.

The water in my beaker had already started boiling. I placed the supplied white cloth between my palms and tried to lift the heated beaker. My hands performed the necessary procedure but my mind was somewhere else. I was wondering how much more time it would take me to complete my artwork. It had been due for a week now, and I still had much left to finish. When I had told my art teacher that I wanted to draw an army of ants, her face dropped suddenly.

"Ants?" She looked at me, uncomprehending. "You're going to draw ants." My art teacher was thin, had a raised, pointy mouth, like a bird. She also had a heavy lisp. "Are you *thssuure*?"

"Yeah." I nodded. "I really want to focus on the ants' details. A microscopic vision."

"How will you make that go beyond—how will it *tranttthscend* beyond two black dots?" Her arms widened in mock artistic flair.

"I'll use the maximum zoom on my camera and find a good scene to picture. Then I'll draw from the picture."

She blinked at me, shook her head. "Artists don't just draw from the picture. They *thhransform*!" A pause. She considered. "Okay, I'll *trusttth* you. Just get it in within the week. You're already a week behind."

"You won't be disappointed," I bleated, wondering when the last time was that I even used my camera.

So while the rest of my art class scurried to Mohenjo-Daro to take pictures of historical buildings, I ambled my way through my back garden, trying to find as large and grotesque an ant as possible.

I spread out crumbs on the damp soil, and waited. Minutes ticked by. Then half an hour. Eventually, her (or his?) highness—a big black queen ant—strolled out of a pore in the soil, and heavily made her way to the biggest crumb of all. She was bulky and menacing. I took a shot just in time; she had mounted the crumb with her threaded-legs against the backdrop of a jade plant. A warrior mounted victoriously over a killed enemy at battle. Now I just needed to get that image down in brush strokes.

All of a sudden, I was jarred out of my daydreaming with a large thud and a surge of pain. *OWWWWWW*. I looked down and saw the edges of my cloth had made contact with the tip of the flame. Within seconds the edges had turned black and curled inwards. Another fraction of a second and the entire cloth blazed with fire. I screamed hoarsely and dropped the cloth on the table. A shaking hysteria came over me and I tried putting out the flames with my hands, trying desperately to curb the fire. Pain shot up my hands like sharp daggers. I felt the raw, exposed flesh of my fingers swell and leap up, like the flames had.

The fire subsided quickly. It was like dynamite action; a loud piercing bang followed by sudden, stealthy silence. Smoke crept up into the air and danced around me insidiously. The air was now filled with the smell of burning charcoal and burnt flesh. I let the mist surround me as I stumbled on my two legs, dazed, like a Sufi entranced in his mystical music.

3

From somewhere distant I heard my parents being phoned. I was sitting perched up on the crisp white sheets of the sick bay bed. I swung my legs to and fro beneath me. I stared at my hands, disbelieving. They were wrapped up in acres of bandages. My fragile hands had transformed into two beefy paws, looking like wads of toilet paper wrapped up in never-ending rolls. My hands were lubricated with oily medication. Good, I thought. It would prevent my skin from desiccating like a sun-dried leaf.

I did remember vaguely how I was brought here. I didn't faint immediately; I had more or less phased out into numbness, consciously dead but still on my two feet. I was carried here by someone, but I couldn't remember who it was. All I recalled was that I was in assuredly strong hands; they lulled me into a sense of security so that I let myself go, and stopped struggling to remain conscious. I remember indistinct voices of other boys and girls running after me. "Oh my God . . . is she going to be ok?" My friend, Natasha, had been so shaken up, she started crying. Her howls resounded in my mind like echoes from the bottom of a long tunnel. It was like viewing a dark, dismal movie and realizing you were in it.

No one was allowed to see me now. I was partially glad. I didn't know how to face everyone's concerns in this condition. It wasn't only my hands that were numb. My brain had been dulled, too. I was still struggling to absorb what had just happened. Was that me?

I wondered if the rest of the class was a bit relieved that the practical had been canceled. It wasn't something they were going to admit, I knew, even to themselves. It was like receiving news that a famous politician had just died; no matter how upset you might be, you couldn't help but be a little excited that your school would be called of the next day. It was a feeling I had experienced myself, when my classmate's mother had died in a car accident. He had been there; he had watched his mother's blood spew across the windshield of a 98' Civic. The boy, Ahmed, was ten years old at the time, and was shopping for *Eid al-Fitr* cards with his mother. *Eid* was a day at the end of the holy month of Ramadan that marked the end of the month of fasting. It was a joyous day. A day of celebration. The equivalent of Christmas. People handed cards and gifts to each other, distributed sweets. The air was indeed heavy with festivity when Ahmed and his mother crossed the street after buying their Eid greeting cards. And then the car rounded up the corner. At fifty miles an hour it hit the mother straight on, while Ahmed lagged behind her, shocked.

I had thought that I would feel a torrent of pain if I were to come across Ahmed in school. But when I did confront him, face-to-face, the only thing that I could remember feeling was relief; relief that it wasn't me who had been bereaved of a parent. Not on that day.

Moments later my mother arrived at the doorway, her face terror-stricken. She sat next to me and clutched me in her arms, murmuring incantations under her breath. I tried to explain what had happened, but she silenced me. "I don't want to hear a word," she rasped, rocking me in her arms like a little girl. "Just lie down and relax. Your teacher will tell me what happened." She then turned beseechingly in the direction of the nurse, who repeated the entire story that I had provided her with.

"But what dangerous laboratory apparatus you have!" She started, her eyes widening in amazement. "Any carelessness could result in third degree burns! If it was Ayla today it could easily be anyone else tomorrow. What responsibility is the school willing to take for this? None?"

I was lying down flat on the bed now. From a sideways view I could see my mother seated opposite the nurse. Ma's back was turned but I could see the sheer alarm on the nurse's face clearly. She said nothing but wore an expression of helplessness that wailed, "I did not decide the safety rules of the biology laboratory. I am the wrong person to be discussing this with!"

"It was my fault, Ma," I yelped weakly. "I didn't follow instructions properly."

My mother conveniently ignored me and went on, "Children are always liable to make mistakes. But the school still needs to guarantee their safety. What will Ayla do now?" she flailed her hand in my direction. "How will she write without any hands?"

Perhaps the brain-block had numbed my senses to this realization. I was practically handicapped now. A cripple. How would I turn knobs, hold the phone, carry my backpack? How would I eat?! I shuddered as images of helpless old people in homes raced through my mind.

Would I have to be fed by my mother, like a nurse and a paralyzed victim? Or would I need a "helper" with me at all times, a caretaker to open doors for me, to comb my hair, to wash my face and brush my teeth for me because I couldn't grip the handle of a toothbrush with those massive paws?

Maybe the caretaker and I would soon grow inseparable, like Siamese twins. We would have to sit at the same desk (she writing my notes for me while I dictated), visit the same bathroom and share the same bed. She'd be right by my side, punching numbers into my calculator and handing my notes to shopkeepers. She would do so compliantly, without a word. I would then become so reliant on her that I'd find it hard to function by myself, even when my hands healed. I'd forget how to hold a fork with my hand after loss of practice, forget how to type, how to paint. I'd implore her to care for me just a little while longer. We'd grow old together and function as two separate parts of one entity; I'd be the central nervous system, giving out signals to act, and she would be the muscle, carrying out my instructions automatically, contracting and relaxing at my will.

We were walking towards the car now. My mother held my shoulders steadily and directed me towards the door. I wanted to tell her that the loss of sensation was in my *hands*, not my feet, and that I could carry myself towards the car without any hassle.

She drove through the noisy streets silently, but gruffly. I gazed at her from the corner of my eye. She was dressed in a white silk *kurta*—a colorless long, slitted shirt—and *shalwaar*—loose pajamas. She crunched the accelerator with a spiky Manolo Blahnik heel. Her makeup was the only tell-tale of her worry; it had obviously been slathered on in a hurry. Her lipstick hovered well over the lines of her mouth, like leaking paint, and her eyeliner was smudged heavily underneath her lower lids; it had spread all the way to her cheekbones. It reminded me of the time I had smeared kajol underneath my lids with an inexperienced hand, trying to mimic the sultry Cleopatra. My mother had instantly remarked that I looked like a Chinese panda. I ignored her comment and defiantly went to my friend's get-together, looking like I had just received not one, but two black eyes.

And here was my mother, the vanity-devotee, reduced to a wreck. The guilt of being responsible for someone else's grief was unbearable; it picked away at my conscience. If I had a functioning hand I might have just placed it on my mother's arm reassuringly and said, "I'll be *fine,* Ma, don't worry." I had no such option so I tried to sooth her with placating words.

"I'll manage, Ma. It'll be fine. I don't need my hands to do *everything.*"

She gave me a curt sidelong glance and stared back at the road. Were we having a normal conversation, she would have muttered,

"Yes, because ninety per cent of your energy goes into chattering. No hands required *there*." But the situation called for a somber, motherly demeanor. She said instead, "Yes, but it could have been worse. What if the flames had spread to your entire body? Your life could have been reduced to ashes within seconds." A tear escaped from her eye and drizzled down her cheek.

"Don't say that," I wailed, momentarily ignoring my pain to relieve her of hers. "I'm well and alive and that's what counts. It could even be fun with these mummy bandages," I circled them around to demonstrate. "They're like boxing gloves—they'll come in handy when I need to fend off stalkers." I swerved them around and hit in the air. "Bang! Oops, sorry. That was your head I just knocked off." I looked back at her to see her reaction. I had made success. A smile slowly crept up her face and she shook her head. "*This* is why your father and I warned you from taking biology. I still think it was a poor choice. You wouldn't have faced an accident like this had you taken something a little less hands-on, like literature, or accounting."

"Yes, and I'm sure you foresaw me getting severe burns during an experiment when you gave me that advice." I grinned and continued, "Next time I'd like some warning, Ma. A heads-up would be nice."

I was relieved that her mood had restored to normal. She wasn't driving with quite the same aggressiveness as she had been. I could sense her muscles and shoulders easing themselves into the seat. She even ran a red light in her calm state of mind.

"And you're not getting any helper if that's what you imagined, missy." She broke the silence in a smooth tone. "You're spoilt out of your wits as it is. Maybe the non-functioning of your hands will teach you a good thing or two about independence." She then paused, which I could have sworn was intended for drama. I could feel the onslaught of an adage. It was something about the way she took a deep breath and acquired that learned look about her. Adages were what my mother usually resorted to when she was at a loss for words but still fired up to make an impact. "If you are drowning and unsupplied with a rope, only then will you learn to swim to safety." She breathed out slowly.

I sighed. "Okay. I'll deal. Just don't let me drown, please?" With that, we laughed and rode home in high spirits.

4

My first few days as an inert vegetable were not easy. How could they be? Once I couldn't turn knobs or open doors by myself, I realized how reliant I had *always* been on other people. A cleaning lady came to my house daily and did the laundry, changed my bedsheets. The natural state of my room was usually a mess; clothes flung about, plates lying with rotting take-away food in every corner of the room. My dressing table was home to a horde of lotions and potions and perfumes and brushes that came together in one big, mighty muddle. However, I'd always arrive home from school to a sparkling room, no matter what a shambles it might have been just a few hours before. The natural state of my room, with its decomposing food and strewn bed sheets, fortunately never persisted for more than a few hours.

Alia called it "gratuitous pampering." She was right. Unlike me, Alia was self-made, self-subsisting. She did everything for herself, from her dry-cleaning to her shoe-polishing.

"I'd hate to be dependent," she had declared when I asked her how she could manage all these tasks alone. "If I'm reliant on people now, I will be reliant for the rest of my life." It was a weighty statement that

I could have learnt a lot from had I really comprehended it. Frankly, I was too tied up in my vision of blissful, chore and mold-free days to try to follow her grave resolution. I'm sure if her parents hadn't forcefully resisted, Alia might have even taken a day job to pay for her school tuition.

Things were different now that I had no hands. The list of things that I "couldn't do" now included button-pressing, doorknob twisting, sleeping on my side, eating independently, opening mail, washing my hair, biting my nails (I tried through the thick of bandages but failed), bread-toasting, smacking my little brother when he taunted me, spoon-lifting, and so on.

Not having the power to perform these everyday tasks that one never usually thought about—just not being *able*—was terrifying. I appreciated that if nothing else, I would, from then on, value every time I opened the lid of a jam jar with my two hands; my God-gifted, divine two hands!

Fortunately, Alia arrived the second she heard about my accident and eagerly grabbed the reigns of my life. She became my surrogate nanny. I felt like an orphaned baby who had just been picked up by a luminous, wonderful new mother. I would be taken care of now. Alia just about declared as much, and she delivered nothing short of her promise. She painstakingly washed my unruly long hair, fed me cream of chicken soup, packed my backpack and wrote my homework out for me as I dictated. She even slathered on my daily acne lotion every night.

"You can't let this hurdle get to you," she instructed, as she worked through my hair. "Don't stop doing the things that you'd normally do; eat as much as you like and play as much you did. Just don't feel afraid to ask anyone to help you do these things. I'll pick your nose for you if that's what you really have to do, just ask when you—"

"Oh God," I interjected, wrinkling my face. "Would you really do that, Alia?"

"Yes! I'd pick your cuticles off your toes if you asked me to. You know I've a high tolerance for gross things."

I grinned to myself. She wasn't lying. Last year, her little cousins arrived for holiday and, unfortunately, none of them knew how to wash themselves in the bathroom. Alia had effortlessly done it for them throughout that summer. She did it as carelessly as flipping the page of a book. Cleaning my cuticles, then, wasn't exactly a giant leap for Alia.

"Alia, when you were little, did your parents ever spoil you?"

Alia returned a puzzled look. "Spoil me? In what way?"

"Well, you know," I tried to elaborate with my bandaged paws, waving them around weakly. "Doing your homework for you, getting your chores done for you . . . well, just taking burdens off your shoulders."

She didn't seem to understand where my questions were heading. Eventually she said, "My father really spoilt me growing up. A lot more than my mother. When I was younger, he bought me German truffles every day after work. They were these yummy raspberry truffles that you couldn't buy easily anywhere around. But he got me at least five different-flavored ones every week. He'd even save me from trouble with my mother. I loved it at the time. Who wouldn't?"

"So you were spoilt! I'd never guess!"

She smiled shortly. "It was well and good in the beginning. I didn't really even think about it as spoiling. No need to feel guilty, right, if you're being treated like a princess?" She continued, "Then one day I heard my parents fighting. They had been at each other's throats for the past few days, but I never knew what it was over. I was walking towards my room when I heard my father suddenly erupt, 'Do you consider yourself a queen parading about her palace? Remember, you will be nowhere without me! You and the children will go around with a begging bowl once I am gone.'"

I was stunned into silence. She had stopped massaging my scalp.

"It's nothing." She dismissed. And I believed her. I knew that if it had genuinely troubled her, Alia would have said as much.

"And it wasn't a life-changing experience or anything." She continued. "It just made me realize that even if your parents spoil you, it's your *choice* to object. You can get the groceries once in a while, cook meals, clean dishes. My father kept buying me those truffles but I stopped accepting them. It just felt like an unnecessary favor. It made me feel weird that I only *mattered* because someone else mattered. Money and gifts, they just stopped meaning as much. I wanted more: I wanted attention and respect."

I stared down at the unfamiliar bandages, my hands throbbing with sensation underneath. A stunning realization sunk in: I hadn't been reduced to a handicapped victim after the burns because, really, I had always been a cripple.

5

It was Monday now, two weeks later. My hands had healed completely, and were bandage-free. That meant I could get back to my artwork.

My art teacher wasn't happy at all about giving me the extra-long extension due to my little accident. But now the day had come. The day my art assignment—my ant painting—was due. My hands were sweating as I handed my painting to my art teacher. *What if she hates it?* My art teacher took a look at my ant painting and raised an eyebrow.

"Not bad." She said. I sighed with relief.

But it wasn't over. She then said, "I will thstill need another painting from you, though." She handed it back to me without a further look.

"Why?" I asked, my lips already quivering.

"This ant drawing is not a realisthhic portrayal," she said, twitching her nose at my queen insect. "The colors are bland. The poses are too cartoon-like. Ants don't mount their food like greedy vultures."

I looked down at my work. So maybe I had exaggerated the stance of the Queen. Her posture had been more passive in the picture. I had extended her hind legs and proboscis, and given her an over-stylized aggression as she triumphed over her crumb.

"But I'm not looking to make it realistic," I weakly protested. "I want to try to bring out the paradox of the ant here. The 'feeble' little insect loaded with a ton of power . . ." I faded out, like a bad-tuned radio, crackling before I lost frequency. It was like trying to explain road directions in English to a Chinese tourist; my art teacher feigned understanding; she even nodded her head occasionally, but we both knew my words may as well have been a different language.

"Yessth, you can interpret it in any way you want," she said dismissively. "My concern is that it's too, well, how do I put this . . ." She closed her beady eyes and pinched the center of her forehead, in concentration. "Yes," she lit up, having found the right word. "It's too flat."

I blurted, "Well, I don't know if I can do anything about that. The paper is flat."

I wished I had kept my mouth shut the minute I let slip that wise-crack out.

She pursed her lips into a thin slit. Her whole demeanor suddenly exuded frost. She grabbed my paint brush from my hand and in an equally chilly tone muttered, "Let me fix thisthh." I watched in silent horror as she dipped my brush, a dagger, into the water and mercilessly jabbed at the Queen's antennae. I was watching my baby being massacred in front of my eyes while I stood, dumb and mute. I suddenly felt as tiny as the feeble ant I was trying to depict.

My teacher prodded the ant's silhouette with new strokes of black blotches, transforming her taut curves into a shapeless lump. And that still didn't satisfy her. After working in her treachery, she gave my painting a long look and shook her head. She then dropped the paintbrush from her thin fingers and said dismissively, "No. It's beyond repair. Start something elssthe, perhaps the thsunset or a lake." She then stood up and marched away to correct someone else's work.

I walked after her. "The what??" Panic rose in my throat.

"The thssunset. Right as it sets over the ocean. Two days. You have two days. No excuses."

Two days. I just stood there. And let her go. I wanted to tell her I had stayed up long nights working on this painting. Neglecting my other homework for days to get this done. That I wasn't ready to throw my work away and start on a *brand new project*! But I didn't say a word. That was me—never wanting to question authority or get into trouble. A people-pleaser. I was also a simmering kind of angry person. I let rage build inside me. Carried it around with me, from one place to the next. My face would turn red and people would ask me what was wrong and I'd say, "nothing." Not a word from my lips. What was that cliché? *Bottled up inside*. Yes, that's what I did, I kept it bottled up. I internalized my angst until it gave me a palpable swelling in my throat.

So I emerged in that same way, like a steaming kettle, from my art room and went to my next class. The good that came about from this whole disaster was that my hands no longer felt quite so numb. They were itching to inflict some serious damage, to crush something. They felt more alive and functioning than they had in weeks. The silver lining in the tempest, I'd say.

~

The color of sunset can never be depicted. That's not to say many haven't tried, though.

Drawing a ball of hot lava is easy. But the residue of deep orange and magenta that *surround* that fiery ball are impossible to capture. The edges of the sun are marked with rich copper, the copper of baked skin when it has been in the sun too long. It even has the same folds as the texture of baked skin: smooth and solid, with deep corrugations like the edges of smoldering rocks. The copper then delves into an almost invisible, tender orange, like the skin of a newborn infant. This timid orange hue meshes into a creamy whale-blue sky: the last vestiges of the day before it recedes into pitch-darkness.

The sun depresses gradually into the ocean, sucking the glorious blue day along with it. It swallows the sky and the birds voraciously, leaving us stumbling about in the dark, unaided, like twitching blind bats.

I had never dared to reproduce the sun in my work. How could you? Is it possible to compress a trembling source of energy onto a flat, empty piece of A6-sized paper? And with my mere paints and my feeble brush, how could I attempt to replicate an already stunning masterpiece painted by the careful strokes of God?

6

"We have guests coming," my mother announced as she walked into my room, with the same pride as if she were declaring the arrival of the Queen of England.

"Ok, Ma." I tried to sound enthusiastic. "Just give me the signal and I'll be on my way when they arrive."

The TV was on in the room. The headlines: *Wheat shortage in Pakistan. Thousands starve.* The heavy summer monsoon rain had wiped out scores of crops. The camera panned to pictures of children lined up in the street, muddied with dirt, their small palms hanging out, begging for food. No tears in their eyes. Just blank, waiting expressions. Another shot of tiny children swarming around a garbage can, picking out dirty orange peels and then loading them into a plastic bag. I recognized the faded gray streets in the background and knew this area was only a fifteen-minute drive from our house.

"I'm going to send the chauffeur to pick up salmon and turkey to serve to the guests; also those special pastries from the Bombay Sweets Bakery. Maybe he can get some pie as well? What do you think?"

"Do we really need that much, Ma?" My voice was low, my eyes on the TV screen. A girl with matted brown hair was dusting off flies from her clothes. She walked with a younger boy to a World Food Program Center.

Meanwhile, we went overboard. Entertaining guests in my culture centered heavily on appearances. *We must not appear cheap, or stingy. Better to go above and beyond than fall short of pleasing your guests.* The seminal question always on everyone's minds: *What will they think?* So we made sure they didn't think. My mother used the finest silver china from Italy when guests arrived.

In fact, Ma had an entire system. The food never arrived all at once. It was served in intermittent sessions. First arrived bite-sized hunter-beef and cherry pieces adorned with carrot slices, each neatly stabbed by a chiseled toothpick. After an intermediary ten minutes or so—after all, Ma didn't want to *distract* guests from the purpose for which they had come—chicken strips with vinaigrette sauce were proffered. Another gap of twenty minutes followed—cue dessert; apple pie or ice cream, maybe some customary *gulab jaman*—small sugary balls of curdled milk, or *jalebi*—deep-fried wheat flour—dripping with sugary syrup. The kind of meal that took a working laborer a week's full of wages to afford.

A hearty, filling meal for a stranger whom we never met before. And Ma would always ask our guests for feedback. "How did you feel about the temperature of the salsa? I feared it was too warm," so that you were reduced to a gourmet critic instead of a casual visitor. Apart from that inconvenience, it was a real pleasure.

My role in the upheaval that accompanied a guest-visit was rather small. I was expected to dress well, welcome the arrivers at the doorstep, and seat them in the guest room. Be polite, courteous. Make an appearance.

I knew that Ma just needed my assurance that I'd be present in time for the guests' arrival. The sooner I agreed, the sooner she'd be able to attend to the more pressing things; light, air freshener, and food. I had no desire to stall her.

"Hmm, ok, no apple pie then," she said and turned to leave. "Oh," she returned a second later. An afterthought. "And don't wear anything too revealing," she stressed. "We have a conservative lot over today."

"Of course," I responded automatically. Humble clothes to please our humble guests. One must be sensitive to other's reservations. I ignored the waging battle within me and robotically smiled. It even looked real.

~

"They're here!" My mother called out, flustered. She rapidly sprayed air freshener around the dining room and lounge. I coughed at the taste of the spicy flowers. "Greet them while I finish up with the food." And she scampered off into the kitchen.

I stood positioned at the main door and realized that I didn't even know who our guests were. My mother hadn't told me, and I hadn't really thought to ask. I knew that we weren't related because as they walked toward me from our front gate, I didn't recognize any of them. The visitors smiled. A rotund, pleasant-looking woman wearing a silk white sari gleamed at me. I was so caught up admiring the smooth flow of the silk as it fluttered against her feet that I quite forgot to smile at the other two guests. A man in a starched cream *kurta shalwar*—tunic and trousers—trotted in behind her. His deep-caramel skin matched that of the older, rotund woman. They had to be mother and son.

And who was the third guest? A darker-skinned girl with alarmingly big eyes and feathery lashes. My gaze lingered on her. She looked like an owl—an attractive owl—with her tiny, round lips and humongous eyes. She was *beautiful*—so refreshingly different! Her lovely features would have stood out even more had she not decked on so much jewelry. There were heavy bracelets and bangles everywhere. It just seemed so, well, out of place. I don't know if I was being presumptuous, but it just seemed like that girl did not *want* to wear that big, glaring necklace.

And then there was something about her that was so familiar. I had seen those striking eyes before. Had I met her at a function, a wedding or get-together, where she had been introduced to me by Ma? Why was she smiling at me right now, knowingly, as if we had a shared secret?

"*Salam Alaykum* (Peace be upon you)," I delivered the customary Arabic greeting. "How are you? Please come inside." I held my hand out to the hall and guided them in.

The strangers looked around the house wonderingly. "You have a beautiful home," the older woman sang as she appraised our white marble floor, the heavy chandelier on the ceiling, and the winding carpeted staircase. Adornments that had taken my mother years to perfect. The guests gaze fell on a miniature statue of a cherub entwined by golden leaves. "And where is this from? It's lovely."

Oh no. I tried to remember. "Quebec." It suddenly hit me. "We brought it during our summer vacation two years back." I sounded jittery even though I was sure of its origin. And she seemed convinced.

My mother arrived as soon as I had seated the visitors in the guest room. She was glowing in her soft-yellow sari. "*So* lovely to see you after this long, Shumaila." Her face crinkled in delight as she held the woman's hand in her two hands.

"I have missed you much—nothing like coming to visit an old friend! And of course, there's the added bonus of getting to meet your daughter," she raised her eyebrows at me. "Ay-la." She pronounced my name in two abrupt syllables.

The lady and my mother launched into soft chit-chatter. From the conversation, I gathered that my mother and she had been childhood friends. They had both gone to the same high school and even graduated together. But then Shumaila had suddenly had an arranged marriage, had to leave school—ah, the "conservative lot," it was all starting to make sense—and both of them had lost touch. Shumaila had had a springing five-year-old son by the time my mother got married. They resumed contact after I was born, two years later. I suppose it felt appropriate. Both of them had babies and motherhood in common. It made me feel a little proud, knowing *I* had brought these two separated friends together. And that springing five-year-old baby happened to be the young man sitting in front of us. The striking girl next to him was his sister-in-law.

My mother then asked about their families' health. She racked off a number of names that held no meaning for me. "Oh, did Junaid sack his cook *again*? Just terrible . . . How is Asma holding up with her chest disease? It's so very sad . . . I heard Saira was thinking about buying a new house. She's moving to the Defense neighborhood."

The conversation finally shifted to the younger girl—our third guest. I had noticed that she remained very quiet throughout the conversation. The boy—was it Hassan?—had been talkative throughout, clearly enthusiastic in the chit-chat. But the girl seemed very shy. She hung her head low, and her eyes glanced downward at her lap. When my mom spoke to her and she raised her face, I saw that her pupils were large and so black that the whites of her eyes were mere specks on either corner, like dotted stars against a black sky. She wore no makeup. But her features were wide and bright, no need for kohl or blush to accentuate them.

I racked my brain, wondering where I had seen her before. It *pains*, it really does, when you see a familiar face and can't identify the moment that you had first landed your eyes on it. It was like sifting through stacks of office files without knowing exactly what you were looking for.

My mother finally expressed avid interest in the young girl. She did so after the chicken strips had been eaten and before the desert arrived, just so there was no chance the girl would be pre-occupied with her food.

"And how have you been, Tanzeela?" My mom warmly enquired.

The girl slowly raised her heavy lashes in that same unveiling way. She smiled wanly and parted her tiny lips to speak. And that's when it hit me.

She was the *bride*! At that wedding. The silent goddess. It was the smile that suddenly jogged my memory. She had smiled at me in that same weak, helpless way at the wedding, when she caught me looking at her. This stranger had silently witnessed my sympathy that night and responded. Maybe it was because I was the only one who hadn't beamed at her fortune as a bride. Even now, I could sense the unease lurking beneath the beautiful dress and the automatically-programmed smile.

"I'm well," she said softly.

"We met your husband at the wedding and he was such a pleasure to talk to. How is he?"

"He's well, too. He's been away for a few days, traveling for work."

"Ah—the husband is away and the house is your fort now!" My mother joked. "That must be a nice feeling."

"It is—"

"Tanzeela has been great around the house." Shumaila—Tanzeela's mother-in-law—suddenly interjected. "She cooks better than anyone at home and directs all the staff; the cook and the gardener. In fact, she has just redecorated the living room. She runs the show now. I just step aside and watch." Her voice was heavy with pride at the domestication of her daughter-in-law. Tanzeela was looking down at her palms as she said this.

"I'm so happy the house feels so full now," my mother said warmly.

"It feels full, but we would love for it to be even more full." Shumaila beamed and looked at Tanzeela. Without any hesitation she said, "Now all I hope for is a grandson to complete our family. With the grace of God—*Insha'llah*—our wish will also come true."

There was a pause. All of us had picked up on the gender-specific word. *Grandson*. Tanzeela's cheeks were red now.

My mother laughed lightly to diffuse the situation. "It is always a pleasure to have children in the family. These newlyweds must want a break from the madness of the wedding, though—hasn't it been only a month since the wedding?"

"Yes. But you know, it's never too soon to start thinking of a family." Shumaila again jumped in before her daughter-in-law could speak.

"Within ten months of my own wedding day my son was born. And then a year later, my second son. What parent wouldn't want the same blessings for their children? A new son, Insha'allah, and many more children to come. And then Tanzeela is already nineteen years old. Time flies by quick, doesn't it, Ambreen?" She looked at my mother with wide eyes. "One has to begin thinking of a family while one is young." Shumaila said this lightly, as if this was just the natural course of things, and as if her daughter-in-law was not in the room with us. Tanzeela's cheeks were still flushed.

Shumaila then turned swiftly to me. The same beaming smile. "How old is Ayla, again?"

My mother said slowly, "Seventeen."

"Main sochti hoon is ki bhi mangni kara do." Shumaila said in Urdu. *I think it's time you think about getting her engaged.* Again, spoken as if I wasn't in the room.

"Oh no, no, she's far too young, now." My mother laughed, clearing her throat and looking at me. I could see how much my mother was straining to be polite.

This was not a necessarily new conversation. Within our community, our family was considered "liberal," and our views on education raised eyebrows on more than one occasion. My mom had once told her good friend at a party that she wanted me and my brother to go to college in America, and have a degree and a career. Marriage was nothing to be rushed into, she said. Her friend responded coolly, "That's nice." She then said, with pride, "My daughter was engaged before she even applied to college. There were just so many suitors, and all from such good families. My husband and I had no choice but to accept one of the suitors and within no time, there was a wedding to arrange. It goes without saying, college soon left her mind altogether!" An off-handed wave accompanied my mother's friend's laughter.

Other supposedly "lenient" parents in our circle were kind enough to let their daughters graduate before accepting a wedding proposal on their behalf. One of our uncles had called up his daughter conveniently when she was in her first year at Cambridge University and asked her to come back to Pakistan immediately because he had a accepted a proposal "that couldn't be turned down." He informed her she would be married to a stranger in six months.

"Ayla wants to go to college," my mom said to Shumaila. "Don't you?"

"Yes, I just took my SATs and am starting to apply to colleges," I said.

Shumaila looked nonplussed. "Colleges in America?"

"Yes. I'm applying to schools all over the country. I want to study liberal arts." It gave me a little pleasure in challenging her.

"I see." Her expression conveyed her disapproval. "Tanzeela was also about to go to college." She waved her chin in Tanzeela's direction, who was now looking at me with curiosity. "But her parents decided it would be better for her to marry now. Good proposals can't wait, you know. And as it is, education can always come later," she said easily.

I could barely contain this anymore. Why wasn't Tanzeela saying anything, standing up for herself? Her shoulders were slumped and she looked defeated.

"Marriage can always come later, too," I said. As I said this, I could feel my mother's eyes on me, disapproving me for challenging our guest, but I went on, "After someone has rounded out themselves and learnt about the world. Don't you think, Aunty?" My voice was sweet, conversational, belying the indignation within.

"*Beti*," Shumaila said this word—child—with emphasis, putting me in my place. "I know women who have spent their whole life on education, and have nothing to show for it now but their books. They are too old to even consider marriage. They are wasting away. That's not what you want for yourself, *hai na*, right? Go to America, see the world if you want to. But then come back home. We all have to. I know many girls who go abroad, have some fun and come back to their destiny. After all, you can't forget your roots, beti."

I took a few seconds, let what she had said sink in. Finally, I said, "Don't worry, Aunty. I won't bury myself in books. I really wouldn't want to waste away." I don't know if she sensed the sarcasm in my voice.

My mother stepped in before I could pipe up again. "We're very proud of Ayla for doing so well in school, *masha'Allah*. Only good things will come, I'm sure."

With that, we went back to discussing other subjects. Finally, Shumaila said it was time to leave. She warmly insisted we return to visit her family at their house. I shook Tanzeela's hand as she was leaving the front door and exchanged a smile with her. "It was good to see you again," I said.

"Thank you for having us," Tanzeela said as she turned away to join her mother-in-law. She said this in an almost an indistinct whisper, a baby nightingale crooning weakly before it was taken from its nest and heaved into a cold, entrapping cage.

7

The next day, on Sunday, I met a boy. At the beach. This boy would eventually become my undoing; he would lead to the unraveling of my life and that of Alia. But I didn't know this at the time. At the time all I could think about was the beauty of the sunset.

A postcard picture—salty beach, beautiful, fiery sunset. Using paintbrushes chipped with overuse. Sky blotched with candy-floss clouds. Salty. A sketch was made, and then torn. A stranger approached. The sunset melted in agony towards night.

Wasn't it agitating when some weighty event—the death of a loved one, a heated fight, or even a rollercoaster ride—suddenly broke your mundane routine, and once it had worn off and you were sitting by yourself reflecting on what had just happened, you couldn't seem to remember a thing? Yes, you knew the basic *gist* of what had happened because, after all, you were there, but when you tried to recall specifically, the actual trigger of the spark, when you tried to relive the scene in your mind, you were left blank.

It had happened with me in the past. A heated spat with my younger brother, Asad. I tried to tell Alia on the phone how the fight had begun, and what had happened. But I couldn't recall a thing. Did the rush of adrenaline that seeped through your body when you were angry numb your other senses? Your sense of memory, awareness? Perhaps.

I only recalled snapshots that day. I had gone to the Karachi beach at two in the afternoon to paint the sunset—as my art teacher had demanded. I was wearing ugly sunflower flip flops and walked around with paintbrushes in one hand, green paint dotting my arm.

My mother was fairly lenient about letting me go out in public, alone and unaccompanied, as long as I had my chauffeur with me—"keeping guard," so to speak. For a fair majority of women in my country, going out unaccompanied was not the norm. It was far too unsafe. Karachi was a big city and crime could occur anywhere, even in the nicer, sheltered neighborhoods, and sometimes it did. Our own house was robbed back in the early nineties, when I was just a toddler. Alia's parents were mugged in broad daylight sometime back, outside their home.

Crime could truly happen anywhere. Running or jogging out on the street was not an option growing up. It was far too dangerous. Not only was it unsafe, it attracted unwanted attention for a woman. Any demonstration of sexuality, even overt demonstrations of skin—wearing a snug T-shirt with bare arms, or Capri pants that exposed the leg for example, would often invite leering looks and stares from men. Wearing shorts was completely of the question. My mother often said that the best thing for a woman was to go around unsuspected in public.

Here I was though, at the beach. I was by myself but my chauffeur was parked only a quarter a mile away, within close "seeing" distance in case anything happened to me. I wore jeans and a long shirt with a *chador*—a large shawl draped around my shoulders.

It was bustling hour at the beach. Camels walked around easily on the sand, tethered by turbaned men in flapping outfits. For one hundred rupees—the equivalent of a dollar—you could ride a camel for ten minutes along the ocean shore. Feel like an Arab in the hot dessert.

Men were manning kite stands, candy floss stands, handing out popcorn and pistachios. It was a hot time of day and women were timidly walking in the water. I saw a group of about five women lift their black *burqas*—complete head to toe coverings—around their ankles and giggle as they made their way through the warm, salty water.

I stood on the sand, lost. The wind flapped against my large, empty drawing paper. I roamed around with my watercolor tools and my water and tried to find an angle from which the sun looked most vivid, cursing my art teacher under my breath for ruining my weekend. Finally, I found a spot and ran to it like a dog to a bone to mark my territory before it got stolen.

Oh no. I stopped to a halt as I realized someone was already there. A boy, about my age. He was sitting cross-legged right before the shore, gripping a camera with a broad zoom lens and squinting his eyes at the sea, as if waiting for something to happen. He caught sight of me with my bright shoes and empty paper and something in him seemed to twitch.

"Are you painting something?" the boy with the camera blurted out. He seemed intensely curious. In that one move the ice had been crushed. We were no longer total strangers.

"Yes," I said. My head was filled with my ma's voice now. My mother told me—as most mothers do—that it was never a good idea for a girl to talk to a male stranger, not when you were alone. It did not look nice for a girl to approach a strange boy and make requests of him. What if the boy took her innocent remarks suggestively and harassed her? And what was a young girl like that doing strolling along the beach *alone*, anyway? *Chi chi, tsk tsk, it had to be her bad upbringing.*

Before I had a chance to say anything else, the boy said, "You can sit here, I'll move." His eyebrows creased, almost apologetically.

I looked around me. The group of women in *burqas* were in the distance now, still giggling and playing with their veils. The camels were trotting along, and away. All was quiet. Only the lapping waves, the shrill seagulls, and the dusty sand everywhere to judge me.

"No, it's okay, you don't need to move," I finally said, and settled myself a few feet away from him.

Looking back now, I can't help but wonder what would have happened had I never stuck around. Had I shaken my head, tucked my A6 sized paper under my elbow, never met this boy, ignoring his soft voice behind me, would things have turned out completely differently?

"You're a painter, are you?" The wind carried his voice to my ears.

I was facing away from him so I craned my neck and nodded, "Yes."

His eyes were still set out to sea, his camera clutched in his hands. Like a lost boy, I thought, as I sketched the outline of the sea.

He did not speak after that. I plunged into my work completely and fully. Colors stained my blank page. The water made little weak folds on the crisp paper. My mind drifted back to the events that had occurred yesterday. After the guests had left, I had buttonholed my mother and asked her everything I could about the distressed bride. What was her background? How old was she? And what was her husband *like*? But my mother couldn't give me much.

"She was brought up in Lahore. I don't know where she studied but she was given a very good offer by a college, the London School of Economics, I think it was. Her husband . . . all I know is he works for some multi-national company as a chartered accountant. He's stationed in Islamabad for the time being so he only manages to come on weekends. They're very well off, though . . . Arranged marriage . . . He's in his thirties, she just turned nineteen. That's all I know. I can't probe any further into their marital affairs!"

"But why is she so . . . *sad*?" I asked my mother, as if she'd know the answer.

My mom responded, reasonably, "Marriage can be tough in the first few weeks. It must be a big change for her. She must be really overwhelmed." And she put it down to that, as simply as reading off a sentence in a book.

I wasn't satisfied. I wanted to talk to this girl myself, however absurd it seemed. But I couldn't tell my mother that. I'd need to think of a way to—

There was a sudden shuffle behind me. A voice drifted, "I'm sorry to interrupt you, but do you think you could shift to the left for a minute? I'm trying to take a picture of the ocean." I judged his expression by his voice. It was sincere, earnest. I didn't even mind that it had derailed my thoughts.

I crept to my feet, and moved two more feet away, giving the boy room to snap his picture. This time I could see him. *Really* see him. He was bent on his knees, gripping the camera body in his hands. His eye—the eye that I could see—was squinted shut in concentration. I looked at the color of his skin, wondering how I would render it on paper if I had to. I'd need to mix red and orange, no water, with a slight tinge of blue. I'd end up with a chalky brown. I'd finally add a violet-purple—again, no water—to bring out the deep brown of his skin. His hair was long and unruly, tossing about and dancing in the wind.

He did not click right away. Countless shifts of the camera in different angles, much zooming and moving. What was he taking a picture of? I looked. A distant boat was visible in the sea. Against the backdrop of the sunset. I'm sure the zoom managed to capture an even clearer vision of the scene. I heard the faint *click* of the shutter.

"Are you a photographer?" I asked without thinking.

He seemed taken aback. Not a word had been exchanged between us for over an hour. For a moment he looked as if he had quite forgotten how to speak. Then he seemed to regain himself. "Yes. More of a Sub-Zero. I freeze moments." He didn't smile at his joke. His expression did not change at all. I smiled nonetheless.

After a pause he continued, "The beach is just beautiful, don't you think? It's a *canvas*," he added, looking at my painting, "of opposing landscapes. The sea, the sand, the sky. And it's put together quite strangely, right? The sea is a symbol for life and it merges with coarse, desert sand at the shore." He pointed ahead. "The fertile clashing with the barren. So strange. And if you look further upwards," his finger now moved slightly higher, in the direction of the horizon, "you can see the sky meshing with the sea. Everything is so—*connected*. And because we're sitting here on the sand, we're linked to the skies as well. Can you imagine?"

"All creations bound together," I marveled aloud. "It's pretty amazing. We humans consider ourselves so far removed from nature, but we're both so connected. We derive from nature."

"And to nature we return. Buried under damp earth," he looked down at the coarse brown sand. "Our bodies are left here, and our souls depart heavenward. A bit of us here on Earth, a bit of us in the sky."

His words fell like sweet music on my ears. I had never had such a conversation with a boy, *any* boy. Every other one I had come across seemed preoccupied with the usual: drugs, cars, girls. Some often put on philosophical acts to impress girls, I knew that. But not him. These were genuine words, sincere, original. For that split second, I felt like I could bare my soul to him, give him liberty to know my mind.

"So we're both here to capture a moment," he chuckled. "My tool of choice is a camera, yours a paintbrush."

"My ammo is my paint, and yours is your reel of film."

"But look at the world of difference," he took out a picture from his camera bag, a previous shot of a sunset, and placed it next to my painting. "One simple difference between the two images. One lacks imagination, the other doesn't," he nodded at my watery sunset.

"Then why have you chosen to do photography?"

"Because I don't have imagination," he laughed easily. "I just observe. And wonder. I think that things are in their perfect state as they are. Imagination would ruin that, wouldn't it?"

"You seem imaginative to me," I responded.

"Then you have misread me. Another concoction of your imagination." He smiled. "Nature, who creates nature?" A sudden redirection.

"God."

"How do you know?"

"I don't know for sure," I said. "But that's what I believe, anyway. Do you follow a religion?"

"I will follow a religion, one day, when I know enough about all of them."

"It doesn't work that way," I blurted. "You can't just pick and choose a religion like it were an item on a menu."

"Yeah? And give me one good reason why not."

"You just can't."

"Exactly. That's not you talking. That's your society, your education. Not you."

"But it's a conscious decision," I said. "I *choose* to practice, and to believe, when I don't need to."

He looked me straight in the eye. Squinted at me under camel's lashes. "All right, let's put practice aside for a second. What do you *know* of your religion?"

"I guess I know the fundamentals, the basics. What to do, what not to do. Don't drink, fast during the month of Ramadan, pray five times a day."

"What else do you know?"

"Hmmm. General historical stuff. Like the life of our Prophet, how he spread Islam from Makkah to Madina, again more dos and don'ts learned from his life."

"Ok. Let me put it this way. You know who your first Prophet is. And you know who your last Prophet is. Do you know who came in between? And don't just tell me names. Tell me their significance."

I was tongue-tied. "Why do I need to have microscopic knowledge of every historical fact in order to be a follower? I feel like my intention is enough."

"And *that's* the difference between you and me," he smiled calmly. "You take on a religion and then seek to understand it. I understand a religion and *then* choose it."

I had nothing to say. My blood was racing through my body, and my heart thumped loudly. I knew that I'd remember those words, and when the time came and I was safely locked up in my room, I'd consider what he said in great depth, turn it over and over in my head, trying to make sense of it. But not now. I had to move ahead with the conversation. I had to pretend as if those words hadn't made the huge impact on me that they had.

And why did he look so confident? A steady smile played on his face. He was adamant in his belief. And he seemed to have that way that made even the most blasphemous theory sound so, so *legitimate*, and so logical. I knew I'd never be convinced. But that didn't stop me from wondering. Why were his words absurd to me? Because I had never heard anyone declare such sacrilegious thoughts so freely?

I had always heard of atheists. But they had never occupied a specific category in my mind. I regarded them in the same way I did Hindus and Christians; non-believers. Because it was only a question of whether you believed in the one God or not, right? If you did, you were a believer, and if you didn't, you weren't. And here I was sitting before a *real* atheist, in the flesh. It sent a shiver of excitement and fear to my stomach, as if I were seeing a villainous movie character come to life.

"I'm not an atheist," he said, reading my thoughts. "I don't hate the idea of religion. I just need to *find* my religion, whatever it may be, instead of having it handed down to me, like some kind of heirloom."

"And is that what you've been doing your entire life? Searching for a religion?"

"Yeah. I'm trying to find signs. Signs of God. God always makes Himself felt in some way or the other, doesn't He?" He paused, and said slowly, "Sometimes when I look at the sunrise, at dawn, I imagine it to be a sign. God is imploring us to witness his miracle; the birth of day. He performs it every single day, at the same time in the morning. And we always miss it. We're sleeping soundly while God works his wonders. And we only see the sun in terms of what it provides us; its function. It makes the plants grow, it gives us light, warmth, energy. Never do we consider what it truly is."

"A sign of God," I said faintly.

"Yes," he whispered excitedly. "A sign of God. Does it really matter which God it is? Allah, Bhagwan, Ahura Mazda, they're all the same to me!" He raised his hands in triumph. "We're just so entwined in our own religions, busy defending them, fighting for them, dying for them, that we've forgotten to stop and *appreciate* the beauty of God. Appreciate *God* himself."

Our conversation flowed. We moved on to the political crisis in the world; the Islamic Middle East versus the West. "The conflict is really just all about religion; Muslims defending their religion because they're so sure America is threatening its stability. Why the insecurity? I don't get it!'

"I feel like you might be confusing terror with religion," I said. "The real problem is miscommunication. We don't get where they're coming from; they don't understand what our intentions are. Religion hasn't caused this conflict. It's misinterpretation: terrorists failing to understand the true essence of Islam; the West failing to understand the true word of Islam correctly. I read somewhere that misinterpretation is what really creates terrorism and what creates prejudice. When they go hand in hand, I feel like conflict is bound to occur."

We spoke till the baby-pink twilight turned violet. The wind became chillier and blotted the sky in sudden gusts. We talked about Iran's nuclear program, the earthquake, about death and the afterlife. Each disconnected topic seemed to merge into the other smoothly, and swiftly, like big waves merging into the smaller ones at the shore. I was jolted when my watch suddenly caught my eye. It was getting late. I had to make it home before nighttime.

The stars were beginning to appear; faint white pearls in the sky. I looked at the boy and wondered if he had to go home, too. It didn't seem like it. I imagined he came here every day, to just sit in the sand and take snapshots of the sea while the day breezed by.

"I should be leaving now," I said, finally. I fumbled for my paints and brushes. I turned around to gather my painting of the sunset. But it was gone.

I turned to him in shock. "My painting! Where is it? Did you see my painting fly away? I need to hand it in tomorrow! Did you see it?" My voice trembled in the cold.

His expression remained solid. "Yeah, I did," he said slowly. Before I could erupt he said, serenely, "Your heart was never in it. It was a waste." He grinned lightly, revealing dimples.

My heart rate quickened in angst, and then slowed down, and slowed even more. I imagined the boy talking to me while my back was turned towards my painting. I pictured him, mid-conversation, seeing my paper toss away with the breeze, not telling me. And he continued talking, glancing at the paper as it moved further and further away; tossing over the sand and bending with every gust of wind, until it landed on the clay of the shore, and a large wave undulated into the sand, washing away my sunset first, and then engulfing the whole paper in a second wave.

I wasn't angry. Even though I knew I'd receive a battering from my teacher the following day and would quite likely have to start on a new sheet, I felt slightly relieved to be rid of that sunset.

I gathered my belongings: the paintbrushes with the bristles clumped together; the plate of pencils, now disordered; and the palette of paints. I said good-bye to him and started walking back to where I had come from. I wondered whether he saw me in the same way as the paper; drifting away rapidly and unsteadily, further until I was just a speck on the sand.

I was struck by a sudden realization: I didn't know this boy's name. He didn't know mine. I hadn't asked him which school he belonged to. I didn't know his age. *I will never see him again.* And even as the thought stung me, I didn't dare turn around and catch a last glimpse of him. I walked slowly on the now cool sand. I felt like I had entered a different realm and was now walking away from it, away and out into the real world. I was leaving a dreamy setting; a watery-blue sky, misty sand, and a mysterious photographer, posed in stillness with a camera in his hand.

I was walking out of a beautiful painting. But my heart ached to be trapped in it, like the fishing boat in the boy's picture.

8

As Alia and I were growing up, we had been fascinated by how similar our names were. "Ayla, Alia, we're practically name twins!" she had said excitedly, when we were thirteen. She had longed to do something daring with this phenomenon. "We could change the spelling of our names," she said. "Replace the '*y*' in your name with '*i*' and it will become 'Aila.' We'll be Aila and Alia! Oh, what fun! It will confuse everyone!" She roared in glee.

"And why not the other way round?" I argued. "You can replace the '*i*' in your name with a '*y*.' 'Alya.' That will even make more sense." Years on, I couldn't understand why I got touchy over the matter of a simple "y". It was only a letter. But it was one-fourth of my name. And even though it seemed absurd, I didn't want to compromise on one-fourth of my identity. Alia didn't seem to be too bothered about it, though. "Okay," she shrugged. "I'll become Alya." She beamed at me excitedly, perfectly happy to have shed her old self.

For the next two months, we became a rage at school. Alia filled in her new name in school books and tests. Sometimes we purposely left out our last names to confuse teachers. After another month, we'd switch and I'd change the spelling of my name while she kept hers. It

was wicked fun for us to have merged into one. As we gleefully manip-
ulated our names on test papers, it didn't nab at either of us that we
were now almost indistinguishable.

And we were the only ones who seemed to take pleasure in this
name change game. Our teachers became further and further irritated.
They'd mistakenly enter my marks in Alia's record and hers in mine.
We convulsed into giggles when our known-to-be-absent-minded
Urdu teacher returned our tests back one day. She had written on the
top of my test sheet, "Good work, Alia!" On the top-hand corner of
the *real* Alia's sheet, she had written, "Needs improvement, Alya." We
trembled in laughter as we both went up to our teacher and tried to
explain that our names were different. She had tensed her eyebrows in
alarm and confusion, trying to figure out who was who. It was a fun,
unforgettable, moment.

For our teachers, however, it was unforgettable because it drove
them to sheer aggravation. When it spiraled out of hand, they felt compelled to call our parents and inform them of our "unabashed gim-
mick." But by the time that had happened, Alia and I had already given
up our antics. I had told Alia that we had to put a stop to it before we
were punished severely. But that was only a cover.

That day after the Urdu test episode, after the comical aspect
of the scene had worn off, I felt dejected. She had thought us both
Alia. My identity had, in a small but consequential way, been erased
from everyone's minds. What had started off as mere fun had led to
a complete blend of our identities, till we were no longer separate, or
whole.

Once I placed my index finger in front of me, right before my
nose. My one finger blurred into two indistinct fingers before my eyes.
That is what we had become: two indistinct blurs that when seen from
afar, were one. I kept moving my finger back and forth, away from my
eyes and then closer. It dizzied me, but it was a rhythmic movement. A
bittersweet feeling. I didn't want to be half of Alia anymore. I was Ayla!
But that day I felt like a nobody.

Isn't that how every human feels when they perceive a threat to their name? It is that feeling that makes us feel slightly unworthy and compelled to correct others when they mispronounce our names. It makes us feel insecure if someone but misplaces a letter in our names. It tugs at us, like a cold sore, if someone we consider dear remembers us fondly but can't seem to recall our name. Who wants to be remembered without a name? What's in a name? Everything, I thought. It is a birth-given label, like a barcode on every book that, though we may like it or not, distinguishes us. It gives us security. We are living in a globalized world now, where people take on multiple identities as easily as trying out new outfits. Our name is now the only real, permanent truth to us.

It can't be threatened, like our lives can.

Even the names of criminals and bombers live on after they perish. After sixteen years of trying to understand who I really was, trying to assess my character and my flaws, I realized that it was pointless to have a fixed impression of myself. I was constantly changing, my character shedding traits and acquiring new ones, like a cargo handler unloading old stock and taking on the new. But self-discovery could be dizzying and disheartening. It gave me relief to realize that my traits defined me less than my *name* did. I was Ayla. It was that simple. Ayla. That is all I needed to be.

Spring came and sneaked away. The monsoon season had begun. The chill in the air was moist, saturated with raindrops and the sweat of toiling rice farmers. Water flowed in the streets and gathered in giant mud puddles. A month had passed since that day at the beach. And yet every time I went out into the night, I felt as if I was there at the beach all over again. I could feel the same wind sweep over my legs and make me shiver despite the heat. It was a fearless wind, one that surrounded and lingered, engulfed. It had pushed me away from the strange photographer.

"Wow, you are really brave, having a conversation like that with a random stranger by yourself at the beach," Alia said over the phone when I told her about my encounter with the boy. "My mom would have hit the roof if she found out I did that." Alia was a free soul, but her wings could only unfurl so much. She was bound by dogmatic values, perhaps even more than I was.

Alia came from a strict Punjabi family. Her parents were more flexible than other staunch members of the clan, but still firm with their traditions. Alia had recounted numerous tales of how a cousin or an aunt in the family had been admonished when they blemished the family name. Her cousin, Shaista, had been spotted at a coffee shop with a few friends from school; two girls and a boy. Her parents had been outraged, less because they had been lied to than the fact that their daughter had been seen with a boy. Shaista was locked up in her room for a month, unable to go out, to receive telephone calls, to greet guests.

Girls in Alia's family were strongly discouraged from going out and mixing with boys, or even any "loose" girls. The clench of the iron fist of values was far tighter than on most other girls belonging to other sects in Pakistan. Many of Alia's relatives had donned the *hijab*, though most women just modestly covered their heads with *dupattas*. Alia's mother had tried to reform Alia as well; screening her jeans and T-shirts to make sure they were not revealing or tight-fitting, and intermittently going through her phone to find out who she was befriending.

Her mother, Nasreen Aunty, had not always been like this, said Alia. She herself married late, at twenty-six, when the bulk of girls in her community had been wedded at sixteen and seventeen. She had studied abroad, in England, when her parents had given up trying to find suitors for their restless daughter. She had obtained her degree in finance and after five years returned to a hostile Karachi, where even her relatives refused to talk to her. She had wanted to pursue a career, work in the textile industry, but her family came down hard on her.

She was ridiculed and gossiped about to the point where she could not continue any more. She succumbed to the pressure and married two years after arriving home.

When exactly the change came about, Alia knew not. All she recalled was that when she was four years old, she remembered vaguely her mother in silky, flowing trousers and starched shirts. After a few years, during which her parents had heated fights, she recalled seeing her mother only in traditional national costume, the *shalwaar kameez*. And with the change in her dress had come a complete change in personality.

When Alia told me this, I couldn't help but wonder: every time Alia's father threatened her mother, yelling, "You and your children would be on the street were it not for me," every time he cursed her and her position, did she regret having succumbed to the will of her family and abandoning her dream? Did she ever wonder what it would have been like had she ignored her bitter relatives, joined the textile industry, and let her career flourish? When I looked at her tired face during my visits to her house, I wondered whether it had even occurred to her.

So when Alia heard that I had had a conversation with a stranger, a *boy*, all alone, unaccompanied, she was scared for me. It was clearly unthinkable for her, unless she lied to her parents and planned extensively in advance to make sure she would not get caught. "Are you sure no one saw you?" She asked me again. When I assured her that there really was no one there, her tone gradually changed. She then became giddy and gleeful. "What a romantic setting—sun, sea, chirping birds! You're in love!"

"I am? Nah."

Of course Alia didn't believe me. When she finally dismissed the topic, I brought up the mysterious bride who had visited the other day. "I want to know everything about her," I said. "I don't know why, it's a sudden urge."

"What are you going to do once you find everything out?"

"I don't know. We haven't even really spoken. There's nothing I can really say to her." I wasn't sure if I wanted to help her, to talk to her, to become her confidante, or simply to meet her. But whatever the urge was that welled up inside me, it was not just one of curiosity.

"Are you going to make her the subject on one of your paintings?" groaned Alia.

I laughed. "No. Weirdly, though, I do feel kind of inspired by her. By a girl in chains. It doesn't make sense. I don't even know what she's like! But she's so *sincere* about everything she does that I just can't help but be drawn in, and want to know more." After a moment of silence I added, "I sound crazy, you can say it."

"Hmmm. I'd be drawn in too, I guess. I can see it. Just don't pick a fight with her mother-in-law, okay? That woman sounds like a piece of work."

We spoke for a little longer about school, homework, friends, and deadlines, the usual, when all of a sudden Alia sprung up, "So here's a question: if you were given the chance to meet again with either one of them, would you choose to meet the boy at the beach or the mournful bride?"

"You claim to know me," I replied. "Why don't you answer for me?"

"Okay," she said quickly, as if she had been meaning to all along. "And there's no need to feel guilty about it. You're a *teenager*, it's natural to be taken away by the opposite sex—"

"Oh my God, please spare me, Alia."

"Ahh, fine!" she sighed. "You want to meet the boy."

I thought about it. "So even if that's true, it's not going to happen," I said. "I have no idea who he is. No phone number, nothing."

"I think you will," said Alia. I could hear a smile develop on her face. "I feel like there's no such thing as a chance occurrence. You met him on the beach. It was destined to happen. If it happened once, it will again."

"No way," I said. "What are the chances! There are twelve million people in Karachi. Most of the city is just numbers to me, not faces."

"He might be one of the next familiar faces you run into then. I mean, you never thought you'd see that bride again, did you? But you did. At your own house! It was for a reason."

"Alia, it's never going to happen. Not with this guy," I insisted. "We are not going to run into each other again."

~

But, of course, we did. I saw him again, a few weeks later. It happened when the memory of the strange boy on the beach had ebbed away, like the spring had. The memory appeared in brief spouts, usually at night when I lay awake, unable to go to sleep, picking at the threads on my carpet. On those nights, I would try to relive the scene again, then drift off to sleep with the sound of doves and, somehow, the taste of salt in my mind.

It happened during a long, tiring week. On Monday, I had told my art teacher I didn't have a painting for her. She had done everything but yell at me and walked away.

My mother had hired a new cook who knew nothing about cooking. My mom spent many days trying to teach him to make *biryani*—saffron rice—and telling me the cook wasn't really that awful and she didn't mind "working on his potential talent."

On a day during the monsoon season, rain seared the moist air. I had gone out to get my cell phone fixed. It had been switching on and off at its own will for months now. I was driven to the cell phone shop far, far away, in Old Clifton. My phone was wrapped in a nylon cloth, much like a sick animal being taken to the vet. The store was in the midst of a noisy, crowded street. The sound of the honking buses rung out as they sped by. Everyone was busy; workers had places to go, books and watches to sell. Children were selling bags of popcorn outside the shop, discreetly snatching a few pieces from the bags to nibble on.

Inside the store, I showed the shopkeeper the phone. He stopped chewing his tobacco *paan* to tell me that I was foolish to have waited so long while it was in clear need of repair. "You'll get it back within three days," he said gruffly.

"Three days?" That seemed far too long, when I knew the most he had to do was tug at a circuit, or something similar.

"Yes, this will take time," he said in English, looking hopelessly at my cell phone. As he talked, I could see the orange stains of the chewing tobacco *paan* dabbed all over his teeth.

I asked him in Urdu, "And how much will it be?"

"Three hundred rupees." He continued to chew his *paan* loudly.

I knew I was being taken for a ride, but I didn't know what to do. My mother would have feigned shock and burst, "You're crazy! I'll give you a hundred rupees and no more!" But my native-spoken Urdu was very weak. I knew I'd stutter and blubber my way through the sentence, making it impossible not to laugh. And then, it was really stuffy in that little shop, with the tiny hand fan in the corner weakly churning out air. I said "okay" and quickly hurried back out.

Exactly three days later, I went back to the shop. My mother told me to go dressed as simply as I could: "If you wear nice clothes, these shopkeepers will think you're rich and charge you soaring prices." So I went in my oldest white shalwaar kameez. It had yellow stains on the sleeve and a tiny rip at the leg. I made sure not to carry a purse; only a small pouch with Daisy Duck imprinted on it—a childhood present. I was happily convinced I looked penniless. I also felt I had the will to bargain now. I had practiced what I would say over and over in my head. I would look that shopkeeper in the eye, unwavering, and say, "One hundred rupees and no more."

He handed me my phone back proudly, gleaming and recovered. I smiled at how shiny and black it looked; no thumbprints or scratches. Almost brand new. I wondered if maybe he deserved those three hundred rupees after all. Well, okay, two hundred was better.

I didn't quite know how to put it to him. After all, I *had* agreed to the three hundred the first time. I fumbled in my pouch, trembling and produced two crumpled one hundred rupee notes. I put it on the counter, without a word, and waited.

"It's three hundred rupees, madam," he said carelessly, putting my phone into a plastic bag. He must have thought I had just made a mistake.

I didn't know what to stay. All my resolve shattered. "I . . . I don't have any more money." I lied quietly, my entire negotiation strategy gone out the window. I wanted to run out of the store, away from the silence. The pause was torturous; having to *wait* for a response in that stealthy room.

He gave me a pained look. His tobacco-chewing ceased for a moment and his jaw suddenly relaxed. Of course he didn't believe me. He finished wrapping my cell phone into the bag and handed it over, without a word of argument. I felt relieved to be out of the store as soon as I stepped out. What a painful ordeal! I hoped I never had to do something like that again.

I came home and undid the bag restlessly. It had been so long since I had last touched my phone. I ran my fingers over its sleek cover, wondering what he had *done* to it to make it look so brand new. I switched open the phone and ran over its keys. But something was different. The background had changed. It was a picture of a grasshopper on a brick, one that I assumed had been taken from the camera phone. I opened the list of contacts. They were all unfamiliar. This wasn't my phone!

I shuddered at the thought of going back to the store again. And facing him. I considered sending my driver. But then he wouldn't understand, or recognize my actual phone. I would just have to bite the bullet and do it again.

The next day I went back to the store. I tried to look nonchalant, guilt-free as I went in. The shopkeeper looked anything but pleased to see me. He chewed his tobacco fiercely, slish-sloshing it noisily around his mouth. I explained the situation to him, trying to sound pleasant.

"Oh!" He took the phone and tut-tutted to himself. "I must have mixed the phones up. Very sorry. Many of my customers have given me the same phone to repair. It causes a lot of problems for everyone." I silently agreed in my head. "Well, anyway your phone is fixed." He fished around in a cupboard at the back of the store and brought out my original phone. For the first time I gazed warmly at the two scratches on the screen and the rough, faded color. Pleased at the familiarity.

As I sat in the car to leave, I switched my phone back on. The screen froze. This time I was truly livid. Would I never wash my hands off that little store and its keeper? I marched back towards it fiercely. I opened the door of the store, sweaty and exhausted, wiping my face against the sleeve of my kameez.

There was already a customer in the store, his back toward me. He was tall and lanky, wearing denim jeans and a black T-shirt. From where I was standing, I could see tiny beads of sweat at the nape of his neck. His shirt was stuck to his back.

I knew it was him before I saw his face. The memory of the beach awoke from somewhere in the corner of my mind, fresh and alive. The shopkeeper was handing him back a phone that looked like mine. With a grasshopper on a brick in the background screen.

"So sorry, *sahib*," the shopkeeper was saying, in a much more pleasant voice than the one with which he had addressed me, smiling happily to reveal his orange, tobacco-stained, chipped teeth. "These phones always get mixed up. These days everyone has the same phone." The boy smiled. And that's when he noticed me standing quietly in the doorway, in my yellowing white *shalwaar kameez*, and with my now very red face.

"Hey!" The boy's eyes crinkled in happy confusion. "I've . . . I've seen you!" A very different reaction to my mute one.

"At the beach," I murmured, my hands loosening around my Daisy Duck wallet.

The shopkeeper gazed at us, confused, and then busied his hands unwrapping a new piece of tobacco paan.

The boy then walked up to me. "You look so different," he said, but not in an unkind way. He seemed quite confused, actually. A little more chit-chat and then he said, "You know, I never knew your name. It was silly of me not to ask!" He laughed. I was reminded of that day when he had grinned at me, his camera resting softly in his hands. He had become slightly darker since I last saw him. He also seemed a lot taller than he had that day. But he had that same grin I so strongly remembered, when his dark eyes crinkled, setting his whole face alight. Like a little boy, I thought.

"Ayla." I said. He repeated my name slowly, as most people did when they first heard it. But it sounded so different when he repeated it, as if it was new to me. "And yours?"

"Shahaan." I felt a sudden relaxation within me once I heard his name. A face without a name was almost not real. I finally knew who he was now; the mystery had been partially revealed.

The shopkeeper interrupted us finally. He handed back Shahaan his cell phone, wrapped in a bag.

"How much does this come to?" Shahaan asked, reaching into his pocket to take out his wallet.

The shopkeeper smiled graciously and gestured for him to stop. "Not a *paisa*, boss. It was nothing. And you are our old customer, as it is."

"I can't believe he let you off but charged me three hundred rupees!" I said hotly to Shahaan as we got out of the store, explaining how I had been charged three hundred rupees. My initial shyness was wearing off. When Shahaan heard, he laughed and shook his head.

"And see how nice he was with you! Even though I *did* give him two hundred in the end."

"You know he wasn't that way with you because you gave him less money, right?" Shahaan said. "It's because you lied. I know it sounds absurd, but sometimes these little things mean more to people than money, even to strange shopkeepers."

I felt embarrassed, unsure of what to say.

Thankfully, he changed the subject. "So which high school do you go to?" I told him. And he told me his. As we continued talking, I realized that this was the conversation we *should* have had when we had first met. But we had crossed the polite trivia-seeking boundary and spoken about everything else. Did he even remember that day? How he had seen my painting be dragged away into the sea, and had let it go? From the formal way he was talking to me, I wasn't sure if he recalled at all.

Before leaving, we exchanged numbers. It seemed like the right thing to do. And now that I knew which school he went to and where he lived, it didn't seem to be dangerous.

I called Alia as soon as I reached home and told her. She was at a family function, and couldn't talk openly. I could hear an impatient voice at the back asking, "Who is it?" I quickly told her to call me back and hung up. I hoped she hadn't gotten into trouble for that.

Alia called me back an hour later. "Sorry, I was at my grandmother's house. She has a really high fever."

"Oh, is everything okay?" Alia's grandmother had always been nice to me. She cooked chocolate custard for me and sat with us for a while every time I came over. "How bad is it?"

Alia shook it away. "She just had some bad food. It will be all fine in a few days. Now tell me what you were talking about."

I told her everything. I could hear her laughing before I had even finished. "What did I tell you! It wasn't an accidental meeting. It was destined to happen. You had his phone for days! And speaking of which, did you manage to find any incriminating info on it? I can't believe that you didn't go through it."

"Well, there were no messages. Just a few pictures of different things: a shoe, a mug, a butterfly. It seems to make so much sense now."

"What did you say his name was?"

"Shahaan."

She thought for a moment. "His last name?"

"I'm not sure. Why?"

"I think Hassan might know him. He goes to the same school." Hassan was Alia's older cousin. "I'll ask him who this Shahaan fellow is. And don't deny your feelings for him," she told me matter-of-factly. "I always knew you fell for more than just the sunset and the sea breeze that day."

It was Friday now. Ma had talked me into going to another wedding. The whole time I was there, I kept a firm look-out for the bride—not the bride at the wedding, but the one I was interested in. But she was nowhere to be seen.

"Does she ever get out of the house?" I asked my mother in the car on the ride back.

Ma sighed pitifully, as if I had told her a baby tiger had died at the zoo, and said, "It's so sad, you know. What a *waste* of her skill. Shumaila married young and trapped herself, and now her daughter-in-law has, too. It's become a family tradition, hasn't it! I had expected her and her husband to come to this wedding. They're newlyweds, they need to mix around and be seen! But, well," she added as an attempt to redeem them, "Not everyone likes to be under the spotlight. Let them enjoy a private life if they want to."

And that's when an idea came to me. It struck me so fast I had no time to form the words in my head before I asked, "Why don't you call them over to dinner again?"

Ma looked puzzled. "Who?" she asked, as if the occasion had been entirely erased from her memory.

"The young bride. You can ask the couple over for dinner this time."

"What? Tanzeela? But they only came here a month ago! I'm sure they have other things to do."

"Like what?" I burst. "The husband is a money-making machine, and the poor wife—almost *my* age, is sitting at home in a wreck. He wouldn't even let her come to a wedding! And as you told me before, they haven't even been on a honeymoon. They need some enjoyment in their lives!" A deep breath and then I said, "They need your dinner, Mom!"

Ma was both amazed and confused. "I don't understand you." She turned away from me and looked straight ahead. I smiled to myself. The matter had been settled. I knew she would call them that night.

9

"Well I suppose you'll be happy to learn that Tanzeela and her family will not be able to visit today, but they've invited us to their house. Tomorrow." My mother announced on a Saturday morning, entering the kitchen as I was having my morning coffee.

I stopped sipping my coffee. I had recently taken my SAT test and had completely forgotten about Tanzeela over the past week. "That's great," I said. "Tomorrow it is. Thank you, Mama," I added as she exited the kitchen.

She popped back in. "Papa asked me to ask you which colleges you have begun applying to."

I took a big gulp of my coffee. The answer was: none. Let me explain, though. I had fully *prepared* to apply to many colleges. I had written out applications. Completed short answer essays and questions. Looked at shiny pictures of many college campuses that boasted horticulture, acapella groups, and star-rated dining hall food.

But something was stopping me. A nagging fear. Left over from when I was eleven years old, when I first visited America. Summer of 2001. July, to be exact. My father had declared that he had had enough of the Berlin Wall and the Colosseum and wanted a "real" vacation for the family. Our previous summer holidays had all been spent visiting historical, architectural sites: the London Bridge, the Taj Mahal the year before that, and then the Leaning Tower of Pisa. Our albums were filled with pictures of each of us poised against a pillar or wall, the Eiffel Tower or the Hanging Gardens looming in the background. Only dry, postcard photos. Ones that when you looked back at them, were only reminders of how frustrated you were with the cold wind that day, and how tourists kept ruining the picture by walking right across when you clicked.

So that year we all decided to go to Disney World in Orlando. The first thing that hit me when I arrived in Orlando was how different America was from Europe. All, "Hey there, how are you?" instead of nodded, "Good mornings." Everyone always smiled. Even when they had no reason to. At the bus stops, on the subway, in the hotels. And no one stared. Girls walked around in shorts and flip flops and men didn't bother to give a second look.

I knew even before we left the country that *this is where I wanted to be*. Roads were smooth. Conversation between people flowed. Americans had museums where people stared at art all day long. I could be there, too! We had left the country the same month, in July. I was only eleven but I had resolved that I would do whatever I needed to study abroad.

I read up on everything I could about America. The Civil War. Christopher Columbus. Native Americans and the sad history of accession and defeat. I learnt that the country didn't like government mixed with religion. Something called separatism. People could drink legally, unlike in our country. Women had jobs, parity with men in many fields. They walked around with bare, shaved legs. In fact, girls outdid boys quite substantially in American schools.

I was hooked. I wrote a fifth grade essay on "Going to America," painted the American flag in my art class and bought an American Barbie doll that was fashioned after a lifeguard in the TV series, Baywatch. I kept a five dollar bill under my mattress just as a reminder that this trip to

America was not just a dream—that this is what I would work towards. Abraham Lincoln looked back at me from the faded green bill, resolute. Lincoln. Liberty. The bald eagle; a symbol of everything that is great about America.

September of 2001 then came. My brother and I had the TV on and were watching an episode of the American show *Friends*. Ross had just told Rachel he had a new baby boy. The screen then turned blank and blinked, "America Under Attack." This was unreal.

The TV was left on throughout the day, throughout the night. My mother and father were anxiously glued to the screen, waiting for updates. My brother was too young to understand what was happening. He pointed to the plane as it neared the first tower of the World Trade Center and tugged at my Mother's dupatta, asking, "Ma, which movie is this?"

Everyone talked about it in school in the days to come. We discussed it in class, with our teachers, at break time, everywhere. Funnily, while this was all going on, while everyone around me was moved in some way or the other, I didn't know how I felt. I was sympathetic, confused, fearful. *What happens now?*

The world-aware kids in my class talked about how 9/11 would affect America's relations with Muslim countries. The religious ones slashed out against America, declaring the whole thing an orchestrated setup. "Bush just needs an excuse to invade the Middle East and get his hands on oil!"

I didn't know where I stood. I was just shocked that the country in which we had been on vacation only a few months ago, where there were jumbo-sized coke bottles and fruit tarts in all colors and sizes, where people were civilized enough to stand in lines without pushing or cursing, where the store lady was so nice to me when I dropped a mug off the shelf and broke it, where all those radiant, smiling people and sweets were now part of a nation that . . . hated us? I wondered if the store lady would still smile at me as sweetly if I had gone there two months after the attack.

I crumpled my five dollar Abraham Lincoln bill and stuffed it into my closet—where it couldn't be seen.

At the same time, I was confused. I hated that everyone around me was shaken enough to weep for the innocent victims, but barely blinked when a poor child died of malaria on the streets, in our own land. Once I was fired up enough to say as much in class.

While my teacher and the students chatted on about the implications of 9/11, I suddenly shot up, "How come we've stopped looking at the problems affecting our own country before moving on to others?" I was shocked that I had the gall to say something like that. I was only twelve at the time. My classmates labeled me "anti-American." From then on, the religious sect in our school tried earnestly to include me in their ranks; they thought we had the same interests. What could I tell them? *I don't agree with you. America is not the enemy. I'm just angry at our own people. Our people care—they do—they hate to see these lives taken. But they're so fascinated with a foreign land's problems that they've forgotten about our problems here.*

One day I asked my mother, heatedly, if Americans would keep their TVs switched on the whole day if one of our buildings had been attacked. And like everyone had at school, she, too, misunderstood my feelings. "How can you be so heartless?" she asked me.

And when college application time finally came there were still persistent whispers in my school. *You know before 9/11, twenty people from our high school got admitted to Ivy League schools in the U.S. right? This year, only four have been accepted to the U.S. Four! And three of those four happen to be U.S. citizens. Students are being stopped and scanned at the airport—young boys are being interrogated for hours for no reason. Guys with names like Osama, Muhammad, Akbar, they're all being stopped for no other reason than their names match that of terrorists. These are kids! Fifteen, sixteen years old! Forget about applying, dude. Save your energy— go to the U.K. Head to Canada.*

The face of a boy in my class haunted me. A straight-A student. Destined to go to a big name school, we all thought. Smart, polite, a math genius. I thought back to our class talent show and how he had been voted "person least likely to be accepted to an American college." We had laughed about it. The boy's name: Osama bin Waleed.

It was seven years later. 2007. Benazir Bhutto, former Prime Minister of Pakistan and the first female to ever occupy a prime minister role in any Muslim country, had returned from exile back to Pakistan. Elections were afoot. She was Oxford-educated. Smart. Eager to purge the country of militant influence and extremism. Her voice resounded on TV every day now. "I fully understand the men behind Al Qaeda. They have tried to assassinate me twice before. The Pakistan Peoples' Party and I represent everything they fear the most—moderation, democracy, equality for women, information, and technology." Her voice rose sharply. "We represent the future of a modern Pakistan, a future that has no place in it for ignorance, intolerance, and terrorism."

My college applications were still incomplete. I wanted to go to America. But that numb fear remained. *Will they want me? Am I ready? How will I represent my country when I'm there?*

As I was thinking about this, the kitchen door burst open. The new cook, Ishaq, came lumbering in. He greeted me and went back to washing vegetables over the sink. I went back to reading my newspaper, crackling the pages as I flipped them. My little brother, Asad, came running in, poured himself a glass of milk, and went back out. I looked up from the paper for a second, and caught Ishaq looking at me. He had protruding ears and a long weary face. I waited for him to say something, but he didn't. He just stood there, leering at me expectantly. He was almost smiling.

Something within me shook. I put the mug back down on the table, got up and fled from the room. My heart was beating wildly against my rib cage. I hurriedly locked my room and stood against the door, breathing heavily. I sat down on my bed, breathing more steadily now, and held my knees up against my chest. Horrid images flashed inside my mind. *He tread onto the garden as the girl ran around with her ball. The grass crunched weakly under his shoes as he approached her. The happy grin on the girl's face vanished as he stopped before her and picked up her ball.*

My brother must have heard me breathing loudly. I heard him stop outside my door and pause. He started knocking loudly.

"*Aapa*," big sister, "open the door," he cried in his small voice. His yelps grew into loud squeals. I wiped my tears and let him in. "*Aapa*, what's wrong?" He asked. I shook my head and said nothing, but he didn't believe me. "*Aapa*, what's wrong?" He repeated over and over again. I playfully whacked my pillow against his face to shut him up. He picked it up and hurled it back in mine, with more force. We did this back and forth, and soon even I broke out laughing. It was all forgotten.

~

Evening had arrived. The time for our visit to the bride's house had come. As Ma and I rode to her house, she kept looking at me from the corner of her eye, certain that I had a hidden agenda on my mind.

"I won't embarrass you in any way, Ma," I assured. "I won't speak out of line, or ask any personal questions." I flashed her a smile.

She sighed. "Yes, you had better not blurt out anything that comes to your mind. God knows, with all your assumptions about the girl, you've even got me interested." She chuckled to herself.

I didn't really know what I was waiting for, or what I expected to happen. If all went by the rules, we would merely chat over tea and then leave, nothing asked, nothing given. I knew that I probably wouldn't even be given a chance to talk to Tanzeela in private. And even if I did, did I really expect her to pour out her life's worries to a complete stranger?

We reached the house exactly at eight o'clock. Shumaila Aunty, Tanzeela's mother-in-law, answered the door.

"Welcome, welcome," she said warmly, and hugged Ma. She turned to me and a slight hesitation came on her face. Perhaps a memory of our conversation earlier. "Ah, and here's our lovely Ay-la," she said briefly.

I looked around the large house in wonder. A long chandelier hung from a high ceiling above us. Beyond Ma's shoulder I could see a long, winding staircase, with a red carpet. Very Oscar-like, I thought to myself. I silently hoped that we would have to ascend those red-carpeted stairs. Ma's friend, however, led us beyond the winding stair-case and into another room with a high ceiling. White leather sofas with gold piping were strewn effortlessly across the room. Beneath us was a plush, white rug, the kind that I imagined Persian cats sleekly curl up on.

"Please be seated." Shumaila led us to a large white sofa. My mother and she exchanged pleasantries and updated each other on the recent happenings in their lives. I did as my mother instructed and said very little. Shumaila Aunty's son, the young man who had come to our house with her, soon entered and chatted with us as well. Finally, after the tea had been served and we had started to wonder if Tanzeela would ever make an appearance, she came.

She entered the room as silently as a cat, so that I didn't even realize her presence until she was right there before me. Today she looked a little fresher, a little more happy. She wore a soft-cream *shalwaar kurta*, long shirt and trousers today, and no jewelry; no cumbersome necklace and heavy bracelets. Her hair was tied up in a neat little bun. "*Asalamalaikum*, welcome to our house" she greeted in her soft voice. She greeted me as she would any other guest. "Hello, Ayla," she said graciously to me, and sat down. There was no look of silent familiarity, or interest, that she had made to me when she had come over before.

After some time had gone by, Shumaila gestured toward me and told Tanzeela, "Why don't you give our Ayla a tour of the house?" If Tanzeela was uncomfortable, she didn't show it. "Of course," she smiled at me, polite as ever.

She showed me the ground floor of the house; the kitchen and the lounge. I nodded appreciatively where I could, and asked questions wherever appropriate. "What a beautiful painting," I said, stopping at a large portrait of an old woman holding a pigeon. "Where did you get this from?"

She looked at the portrait keenly, narrowing her eyes, and then shook her head, laughing. "I have no idea." We both laughed at that, feeling more at ease around each other. I told her how I felt the exact same way when her mother-in-law had asked me where the cherub statue was from. "And it really wasn't from Quebec," I told her. "I realized this the day after."

She laughed again. "Come, let me take you upstairs," she said. I felt overjoyed at being offered the chance to saunter up the red carpet, up the stairs. I clung on to the railing, trying to assume an air of importance. When we reached the top, Tanzeela showed me the upstairs parlor, the balcony, and finally, her room. It was a large room, with a sprawling king-sized bed, but minimalistic. I almost forgot that the room belonged to her husband as well. I had yet to see him.

"So which school is it that you go to?" she asked, breaking the silence.

"Karachi Grammar" I replied. She raised her eyebrows in surprise. "Oh! We went to the same school then." This was great news. "Which year did you graduate in?" I asked. 2006, she said. She was two years older than me. I tried to remember if I had ever seen her before, around school. Is that why she had looked so familiar to me in the first place? I looked at her bright face, with her large eyes and sweeping eyelashes, but I couldn't remember her at all. As she continued talking, my mind rummaged for an image of her. Little snippets were coming back to me. I remembered Natasha, a friend at school telling me, during a conversation, that a girl in our school had been offered a position in the London School of Economics. But she had turned it down. To get married.

"Were you offered a position at LSE?" I blurted. I just had to know.

Her smile weakened now, and she looked down. "Who told you that?"

"My economics teacher," I lied. "She was raving about how smart you were."

Tanzeela seemed uncomfortable now. She didn't meet my eye. "Yes, I was," she tried to laugh. "But then my marriage got arranged. I had to make a decision." She went silent.

I nodded in understanding. "Well, you put your family first. There's nothing wrong with that." We were sitting on her bed now.

She fidgeted with a crease on the bed-sheet. "Well, there are times when I do regret it." I was silent, unsure of what to say next. She looked up at me. "But there's no going back now, so it's useless to imagine, right?" She chuckled. "Hey, I think I saw you at a yoga class on Twenty-sixth Street, a few months back. Do you still go?" I couldn't blame her for trying to change the subject.

"I haven't been for a few weeks now. Do you go there, too?"

She nodded. "I used to. But I barely have any time. I was thinking of joining again . . ."

"Well, you should!" I piped up. "We can go together if you want. It'll be fun." I lowered my voice and tried to sound more casual. "I was thinking of joining again as well."

Thankfully, she seemed pleased by the idea. "It'll be nice to go with someone," she agreed. "Is next Saturday good for you?" We arranged a date to meet and go to the yoga class.

My eyes suddenly rested on a picture on the bedside table. I hadn't noticed it the whole time. It was a photo of Tanzeela and her husband, on their front lawn, I presumed. They weren't holding hands; standing side by side, they were barely even touching. Even though her husband was grinning, he looked ferocious. His deep set eyes were buried deep in his dark, hooded face. I remembered his thick, meeting eyebrows from the night of the wedding. Tanzeela looked so small and meager next to his puffed out chest and broad shoulders. Like a kid sister, not a wife, I thought. Tanzeela noticed me gazing at the picture and turned to it. There was that uneasy look on her face again. "My mother-in-law took this picture," she said quietly. "It was the day after our wedding." She suddenly turned to me, as if adamant to drop the subject. "I think we should go back down," she tried to resume her cheerful voice. "Before your mother thinks I've kidnapped you."

We went back to the drawing room in silence. I was amazed to see who had arrived since we had left. It was none other than Tanzeela's husband. He sat across from my mother, large and robust, in a navy blue suit. They were in deep conversation. I heard his booming, deep voice and saw his hands move swiftly as he gesticulated. He seemed at ease with himself; confident and in control. He smiled as the two of us walked in.

"Ayla," my mother said. "Meet Amar, Tanzeela's husband. We went to their wedding, if you remember," my mother was looking at me nervously, scared that I'd lash out at him like a disgruntled monster, digging my claws into his designer suit. "Hello," I said, and sat down beside my mother. I was surprised at how friendly he was. My mother seemed completely taken by him. From what I gathered, they were discussing whether smoking should be banned in all public places. My mother was sure that it should. "It is the only way to curb the habit. Allowing kids to smoke in cafés and restaurants is like giving them a license to kill. Themselves, that is."

Amar said that my mother's argument was valid. But banning smoking was a terrible business decision. "Kids these days go to the café to smoke. And they don't mind having some coffee while they're at it." Everyone laughed. "No smoking would mean no customers. Businesses would have to change their entire marketing strategy. It would be crippling."

I could tell by my mother's expression that she was impressed. I already foresaw her telling me, as soon as we entered our car to leave, "How silly of me to have been taken in by your words, Ayla. He's a charming boy. I don't know where you get your ideas!"

Sure enough, that's exactly what she said when we reached the car. She raved about him as if there were no tomorrow.

"But Ma," I tried, cautiously. "Didn't he look a bit, well, fierce? Not in the way he spoke, but just his . . . overall demeanor? And did you notice how Tanzeela went completely quiet when he was around?"

"Poor man, what can he do about the way he looks?" Ma said. I knew the point was to make me feel cruel. It was working, sort of. "Well, I'm going to meet her for yoga next Saturday," I said, trying not to sound calculated. "Maybe then I'll find out how fierce he is or isn't."

"Oh God, Ayla," my mom sounded truly fed up. "What are you going to do even if he does beat her? Are you hoping to save her from her marriage like an archangel, or rescue her from a villain from the castle chamber? This isn't a soap opera, Ayla. You can't interfere with people's lives."

I remained silent for a while, hurt by her lack of faith in me. "She was in my school, Ma," I finally said. "Two grades above me. Maybe she shouldn't only leave this marriage to get away from him. Where she really belongs is LSE. I can tell she regrets not going. I just hate to see a dream like that wasted."

Ma didn't reply for a long time. Then she said, "These decisions are not yours to make." For the rest of the way there was silence.

10

Shahaan called me on Monday morning, when I was fast asleep. My summer holidays had just begun and I had taken to staying up the whole night watching television, reading magazines—basically catching up on all that I had denied myself during school. That meant that I usually wasn't able to wake up before three or four o'clock, usually only after my mother's insistence that I be present for supper.

My phone rang at nine-thirty in the morning. I thought it was my alarm so I swiftly banged it shut and went back to sleep. When the phone rang again, I confused it as part of my dream. The third time that it rang, I snarled and stared, bleary-eyed at the screen. It was an unknown number.

"Hello?" I said. My voice came out a rasping croak, so I cleared my throat feebly and said again, "Hello?"

I heard a laugh at the other end. And then I knew who it was. "Sorry to wake you up."

I told Shahaan it was okay and asked what he was doing up so early. I found out that he had just come from a morning walk. A morning walk? Do people really do that?

Shahaan was wondering if we could meet up sometime soon. "You can bring a friend along," he said hurriedly, knowing that I might be hesitant otherwise. I mentally decided that I would drag Alia along; I was relieved that he sensed that I was uncomfortable at the thought of meeting him alone. So it was decided that the three of us were to meet on Tuesday, in the evening.

I was fully awake by the time I hung up. Knowing that it was pointless trying to go back to sleep, I called Alia and told her everything. She grumbled that it wasn't wise of me to ask her favors after I had just woken her out of a blissful, heavenly sleep. But she eventually relented.

When Tuesday rolled by, I was up and ready to go. I was to pick up Alia from her house and then head on to Old Clifton. When I knocked on her door at 6:30 p.m., she took ages to answer. I steadily drummed my fingers across her wooden door, my knocks transforming into a real, soft beat.

"O-pen up like a good old girl," I sang to the beat of my drumming fingers. "Or I swear I'll leave you behind." I heard her shuffling about inside. This was strange. She finally opened the door and wrenched me inside. "Sorry," she whispered. "I didn't want my mother to see the mess in my room. I was afraid she'd be walking around." She got her wallet and bag assembled. "Just give me a second," she said, and disappeared into the bathroom.

As I waited on her bed, I heard Alia's phone ring from her bag. I went to answer it. It was Natasha. We chatted for a minute and then I hung up. As I was putting the phone back into her bag, I felt something sharper than usual brush against my skin. I fumbled around in her purse until I came across the culprit. It was a box of *Hi-Lite* cigarettes. And just as I thought, it wasn't empty. My guess was that it had been newly purchased.

I sighed and put the box back in. I knew that Alia only smoked when she felt depressed. And even then, it was never more than a cigarette at a time, usually stolen from her elder brother's room. But she couldn't have stolen an entire pack. Something rather significant must have pushed her to go out and purchase the whole box itself. I couldn't imagine upright, moralistic Alia, stationed before a shopkeeper in some gas station store, asking for a box of cigarettes.

Alia quietly came out of the bathroom, grabbed her bag and her keys, and said brightly, "Let's get going!" As we both sat in my car, I gazed at her discreetly. I was reminded of the time my mother was driving me home from school, when I had just burnt my hands. I was trying to look at her and understand her in the same way. But my mother was distressed, and it showed in her gestures. Alia did not look the least bit troubled. She started talking about her literature test; how well it went.

"I found your cigarettes in your bag," I said. "When did you start again?" I tried my best not to sound like a prim schoolteacher, and more like a concerned friend.

Alia didn't seem embarrassed. She looked momentarily surprised. "Oh," she said.

"Well, are you going to tell me what's going on?" I was afraid I'd have to pry it out of her, like trying to wrench off the skin of an onion leaf with a pair of tweezers.

Alia was silent again, and then sighed deeply. "It's been an on-off kind of thing," she said at last. "There's nothing really *wrong*. It's just, you know, my grandmother's been sick for the past few weeks, and so my mother's been in a horrible mood. She's been getting angry at me over the smallest things: my clothes not being hung properly, my waking up late. That's why I didn't open the door right away. I just feel a little better once I've had one, you know."

"You could have called *me*, silly," I said. "What good am I if you need a dumb cigarette to make you feel better?"

"I don't know," she sighed. "Being on the phone is just another habit that my mother's cracked down on. It's hard to call you."

"Is it easier to go to a store and ask for a box of cigarettes, when your driver could easily be watching and tell your mother?" I knew I was being unfair. "Look, I'm not trying to be a pain. I just want it to be easy for you to come to me, rather than have this awful alternative."

Alia laughed. "Well I guess I never expected you to be the type to say 'smoking kills.' Okay fine, you toad, I'll drop the habit." She squeezed my knee to reassure me. And all was normal again. I thought.

We reached the Café at five past seven. I was happy to see that Shahaan was already there. He was sitting at a round table. My happiness faltered when I spotted a filled ashtray on the table. He was lifting a cigarette to his lips and puffing out ringlets of smoke. "My God," I muttered to Alia in dismay. "I need to start hunting for new smoke-free friends."

As we went up to the table and greeted him, he stood up and offered Alia and me chairs. I was wondering to myself whether chivalry could make up for a bad habit when he said to me, "I never got to ask you how your art is going. Still working on the sunset painting?"

"No, I left it. You were right; my heart really wasn't into it." Shahaan seemed pleased that I had realized this. Alia and Shahaan then got to chatting about her cousin, Hassan, and how he knew him. Shahaan and Hassan were in the same school cricket team together, he said, but they didn't know each other very well. I was relieved that the two of them were getting along well. Shahaan had taken care to look good today, I observed. His floppy hair was pulled back, and he was wearing a black, button-down shirt; both quite different from the first two times that I had seen him. He paused, and looking at us both, asked, "Is it okay with you girls if I smoke?"

I was considering what to say, when Alia quickly piped up, "Of course." They both looked at me for approval. I threw my hands up. I didn't want to be a killjoy. "Okay. Majority rule!" We all laughed. "You know," I said, smiling. "I was just in the middle of this heated debate a few days ago, over whether smoking should be banned in all public spaces. And it's funny how the businessman seems to put the wishes of teenagers like you guys," I gestured to Shahaan, "before the welfare of society."

Shahaan laughed and tapped his cigarette over the ashtray. "And why is that?" he asked.

"Because you're their target market," said Alia simply.

"That's flattering," Shahaan said, leaning back. "Let me enjoy this smoke then, knowing I'm putting money in someone's pocket."

The evening went by quickly. We ordered coffee and cheese dip, and granted the waiter a generous tip. Shahaan offered to drop us both to my house. As we sat in his car, me seated next to him in the front with Alia sitting restlessly at the back, I hoped badly that Shahaan wasn't a fast driver. "I think I should duck," said Alia worriedly from the back. "I can't risk anyone seeing me." We all were in fits as she tried to curl herself up into a little cocoon at the floor of the car. "No one will see you, Daff," I assured, in between giggles. Shahaan looked at me, confused. "Daff?"

"I call her Piggy and she calls me Daff," Alia explained from the back. "Childhood names."

Back in eighth grade, Alia once came to school with swollen, red lips. She had accidentally walked right into her door. "What, did you forget that you need to open it to get to the other side?" I had snickered at her in school. Her lips were so large for the rest of the week that I felt compelled to give her a new name that was fitting. Daffy Duck it was; abbreviated to Daff. Her lips resumed their normal size a few days later, but the name stuck. I explained this to Shahaan.

"And what's the story behind Piggy?" he asked.

"I'll tell you," boomed Alia from the back.

My face flushed red. "No, don't!" I squealed at her.

"Why not?" she retorted.

"Because mine is much more embarrassing." I silently pleaded her with my eyes.

"Fine," she sighed and sat back in her seat. "Not just yet."

Shahaan sensed my discomfort and didn't press us to tell him. We reached my house fairly quickly. "Ok, so long," Shahaan said as we let ourselves out of the car. "I hope we can do this again sometime." After taking down Alia's number, he drove off into the dark.

"He's all right," said Alia, as soon as we entered my room. In Alia's terminology, that meant she was more than impressed. "But where was that philosophical streak of his that you were raving about? He didn't seem very . . . deep."

I thought about what she said. No, Shahaan hadn't spoken with the same passion as he had that day at the beach. Maybe it was because Alia was there. And then again, the atmosphere wasn't right; we were in a dark little café, not a sunny, musical beach. He had been polite, yes. But that depth that I had seen when I first met him, the ease with which he described his feelings about nature and art, that was missing. Today he seemed almost . . . well, just like any another boy. "I don't know," was all I could say. "Maybe he was shy. And that was real smart of you, openly smoking at a café like that, like a puffing dragon," I added. "I didn't want to sound like your mother in front of him, so I didn't say anything."

Alia looked down and smiled sheepishly. It was her notorious guilt-smile. "Just once doesn't hurt. I've never done that before, you know. It actually felt pretty good."

"What?" I heaved myself down on the bed in front of her. "Isn't it enough for you to do it in your bathroom at home? Why is it any better?"

"It's just . . . oh, you won't understand. It's liberating; I finally felt free, like no one was watching me. I didn't have to be on edge worrying if I would get caught."

I looked at her helplessly. I badly wanted her to stop smoking. Not only because she could get into trouble, but because it was so . . . out of character. With a cigarette in her hand, Alia was somehow less familiar to me; more distant. I wanted to tell Alia all of this. I wanted her to open up to me; turn to *me* for her worries instead of nicotine. But I couldn't find the words to say so. So I made a mistake that I knew I would regret: I remained silent.

11

The day for my yoga class eventually came. The class took place at the top
floor of Ghazal's house, who was a single mother. She gave math tuition
downstairs and yoga classes upstairs. "What an amazing way to live," my
mother had gushed. "You do your strenuous teaching for the first half of
the day. Then you want to relax and unwind—and yes, why not make
money off it—for the second half of the day. That woman is a genius."

Secretly, I admired Ghazal too. She had made the most of the circumstances, and had done something for herself. I imagined what it
would be like to make pot-loads of money, without ever having to
step out of the house. Ghazal smiled and greeted me from the head of
the room once I entered. I waved to her and put my things on the far
corner. I quickly looked around. There were two older ladies, wearing
tank tops and revealing knobbly arms, clearly exhausted, on two mats
on the left side of the room. There were three other girls, in their late-
twenties, whom I recognized and spoke to occasionally, and one more
girl, Ameera, who was younger than me and thin as a rail, sitting by
herself in another corner. Tanzeela had not arrived yet.

I laid out my mat between Ameera and the twenty-something girl
and sat down. Ameera was on her back, her knees over her head, each

touching the side of one ear. It was a hard position, one that the older girls in the room, and even I myself, envied her for. Ameera's eyes were closed in deep concentration. She was so removed from the rest of us, from the room.

"The crux of any yoga practice is the performance of yoga positions," called out Ghazal from the head of the room. "These are called Asanas." The name sounded wondrous. "We've tried breathing techniques for the first few weeks," she continued. "We're going to try to do some easy positions now." I gazed at Ghazal's taut neck and defined collar bone, draped by her skin like a beautiful painting covered by cloth. Her jugular vein protruded artistically along her neck, disappearing towards her shoulder blade and flexing every time her muscles tensed. The slight depression right above and in the center of her collar bone glistened with mild sweat. As she was showing us various positions, walking around the room to help balance us where we went wrong, Tanzeela entered.

She was wearing white pajama bottoms and a large, blue T-shirt. Her hair was tied back in a ponytail, with a hair band stretched across her forehead. I had never seen her like this, out of her ordinary *shalwaar kameezes*, and smiled at her. She eyed the room and when her gaze rested upon me, she smiled back and waved. First she stopped by to speak to Ghazal, apologizing for being so late. I tried to make room for her between Ameera and myself. Ameera feigned deep agitation at having to interrupt her position to move her mat a few feet to the side.

"Thank you," Tanzeela whispered, settling herself between us. Since Ghazal didn't allow us to talk during classes, we performed our positions quietly for another forty-five minutes. Only when class was over and we had begun to gather our things did we talk. "I almost thought you had forgotten to come!" I told Tanzeela.

"I know, I'm sorry," she truly sounded guilty. "It's a little hard to get out of the house." She looked down and then sipped her water, avoiding my gaze.

I pretended to ignore what she had said. "So," I piped up, "do you want to stop downstairs for coffee or something? There's a coffee shop only next door."

Tanzeela considered for a minute. "I'd love to, but I am supposed to be home within an hour of the class." She glanced at her watch.

I searched her face for traces of fear. "But I guess there's no harm, if it's for a little while." She shrugged and smiled. So we said bye to Ghazal and walked to the café down the road. It was empty, which was a relief. The last thing I wanted was some eagle-eyed relative of hers spotting us and then reporting to her family.

We ordered two iced lattes and a bottle of water.

"So, which subjects have you taken?" Tanzeela asked conversationally. I told her my choices and she nodded. "Wow, I could never do world history," she shook her head.

"Oh, don't worry," I said. "Neither can I." She laughed. I asked her what her choice of subjects was.

I had begun to notice that every time she spoke of school, her expression changed; she stared into space and looked thoughtful, as if it were a truly memorable period of her life, which it must have been. "Economics, accounting, and math," she answered. "I wanted to go into accounting." She smiled uneasily and looked down at her coffee. I wasn't sure how to respond.

"Well, maybe you still can," I blurted.

She looked up with her sweeping, long lashes and raised her eyebrows, slightly amused.

"I don't know much about . . . your husband," I quickly said, "so I can't really say whether he would mind. Would he?" I hoped I didn't sound too tactless, even though I was proud of myself for having wound my way towards the question.

Tanzeela fidgeted with the handle of her coffee mug. She looked up at me, as if unsure of whether to continue, and then said, "If I'm being completely frank," she said slowly, "it's out of the question."

"Oh," I sipped my coffee, my head buzzing. "It's a shame, because you have so much potential." Oh God. There I went again; why did I always sound like a schoolteacher when I least intended to?

Tanzeela scratched her neck distractedly and then said, "Well, I know that when I was young, and people asked me what I wanted to be when I grew up, the last thing I imagined myself saying was 'a housewife,'" She rested her chin on her clenched hand. The other hand drummed aimlessly on the table. She was looking down absentmindedly, when her gaze fell over her watch. "Oh no," she seemed frantic. "We've been here for half an hour! I really should get back."

We asked for the check and quickly left the café. It was getting dark now. I could hear crows busily cawing their way towards their trees, mosquitoes buzzing around the dusky air. Tanzeela and I exchanged numbers before she quickly disappeared towards her car. "See you next week!" She abruptly turned and called for her chauffeur.

She then turned and left—a crow hurriedly trying to reach her tree before night fell.

⁓

By the time I came back home, it was a quarter to eight. I felt sticky and hot and wanted to jump in the shower right away. I thudded up the stairs and into my room. As soon as I had opened the shower, I heard sharp thrusts at the door. "Oh God," I moaned to myself. If it was Asad asking to play monopoly again, I was going to clobber him. I quickly fastened a bathrobe around myself and whipped open the door, ready to turn my little brother away.

But it was not Asad at the door. It was Ishaq, the cook. I was least prepared to see him standing there. I suddenly felt naked, exposed. He looked dazed as he always did; half-awake. I cringed at that sly, little smile on his face.

I tried to sound assertive, unmoved, when I was suffocating on the inside. "What is it?" I asked him curtly, in Urdu.

"*Begum Sahib*," he said in a soft drone. He was holding out something very familiar-looking in his hand. It was . . . my cell phone. How did he get it?

"You left this in the car." The sight of his fingers wrapped tightly around my phone made me recoil. I quickly grabbed the phone from him and slammed the door shut. I didn't hear the sound of his footsteps leaving. Was he still standing there?

I didn't want to get out of my bath. I shivered in the warm water, my eyes closed. I couldn't get the image of what had just happened out of my mind. While I stood there, I had felt his eyes pricking all over me, as if I was being bitten by little termites. I was unable to get over that feeling; my skin pricked and itched all over in the water. I didn't want to leave my room; I never wanted to face him and those hooded eyes ever again.

And yet, at the same time, I knew I couldn't tell my mother. I had little to pin against him. He had simply come and given me my phone; that was how it would look to any outsider. How could I explain that it was the way he looked at me, slowly and deliberately, that made my insides churn? She wouldn't understand. Not until he actually said or did anything improper. This made me feel even more aggrieved.

As I was sitting on my bed, thinking about this, the phone rang, breaking the buzzing silence. It was Shahaan. I answered it on the fourth ring. "Are you alright?" he asked. "You sound as if you've been crying."

I tried to sound as cheerful as I could. "Everything's fine," I said. "I'm just exhausted."

"I don't believe you," he said easily. "But I'll wait till you're ready to tell me what's wrong. If you're not willing to now, that's fine."

I remained silent, lacking the energy to refute him.

"Well, I wanted to deliver some good news to you," he said. "There's going to be an exhibition at the Marriot Hotel next week. Some new, young photographers are displaying their work. A few of my pictures will be displayed as well. I was wondering if you and Alia would like to come."

"Your art work at an exhibition? That's amazing, Shahaan. Congrats!" I said, feeling a little better now. "Your very own exhibition!"

"Well, not completely," he laughed. "I'm just one in the huge horde of photographers there. But anyway, I've called some friends from school and I'd really like it if you two would come. It's next Tuesday. 6 p.m."

"I'll be there," I said. "I'll talk to Alia about it. I'll finally get to see some of your work now." I was genuinely looking forward to it.

"And I hope to get to see some of your work, too. Soon," he said.

"I am actually working on a new painting now."

"Really, what's your subject?"

"I guess you'll get to see it," I teased, "when it's complete. But I can firmly say I've put everything into this one."

We talked for a few more minutes and then hung up. The image of Ishaq had more or less been erased for the time being. I called Alia and told her the news. She said she could most probably make it, if she was allowed out. "I've had family over for the past week," she groaned. "I really need some time away." I could hear loud voices behind her.

After we spoke, I lay back in my bed and started wondering what Tanzeela was doing; if she had gotten into trouble for arriving home late. I hoped that she would be allowed out for yoga classes next week. I fell asleep on my bed, my last thoughts being of a dead kitten I had seen in the middle of the road; its insides chewed and splayed over the road by an eagle.

12

When Alia was ten years old she used to write songs. She would never admit this to me, and to this day she doesn't like talking about it. Indeed, she had not revealed anything about her song writing to me until I had pounced on an old journal in her bottom-most drawer, thinking that it was a diary. She called, "I'll kill you if you read it!" Finally, when I escaped to her garden, to a spot where I knew she wouldn't find me, and sat in the dewy, soft grass, out of breath, I was able to open the mysterious diary and peer into her soul.

To my dismay, there were no heartfelt entries bursting, "Dear Diary, I hate myself and everyone around me." Instead I found, in indistinct scrawls, written songs. I had thought they were poems at first; with the perfect rhyme scheme and ordered rhythm. But then at random instances throughout the page were written "Chorus". There was a song called, "Dripping Water," and a shorter song called "Handicapped Girl." I read the song, curious to see how far my friend's imagination had taken her. The chorus read:

> *Oh, Handicapped Girl, please don't cry,*
> *You're alone in this world, by and by.*

You're life's a blur, full of misery,
I wish you were near, happy and free.

I was taken aback. The sounds of chirping birds and crows in the garden suddenly faded. At that moment, I wondered whether Alia was truly . . . distressed. Why would she write about a handicapped girl? I wondered. Had she seen some TV show, or witnessed a crippled child at the traffic signal?

As I read on, I became even more saddened: the lyrics turned more graphic and vivid. I didn't want to read any more. When Alia had finally found me, I offered her the journal back to her without a word. I wanted to ask her what she felt when she wrote these songs; my God, she was only ten years old. "So what did you read?" she asked, frowning.

"I didn't know you wrote songs," I said, trying to pretend like I hadn't just pounced upon what I had.

"I write some now and then," she said easily. "It's a good way to, you know, let out your feelings." I shuddered to imagine what kind of feelings Alia might have had to have written about a girl whose wrists had been sliced off by her own parents.

I'll wait, I thought to myself. I'll wait until a day that she's ready to talk about it. But in my heart, I knew I was too scared. Scared of knowing what I'd rather not know. It was silly, I knew, being afraid of my own friend's thoughts.

It had been six years since that day in the garden. I was still trying to find the right day.

～

The monsoon season was now in full throttle. Rain slapped against our windows. Trees were shaking. Leaves dropped quickly and littered the streets. The day for the exhibition came sooner than I expected. Alia arrived at 5:15, wearing a green, cotton *shalwaar kaameez*. It was very unlike the clothes I was accustomed to seeing fashionable Alia in. I gave her a questioning look. "I didn't want to create a scene in the house," Alia explained. "My mom checks what I am wearing a whole lot more when there are family and relatives around."

"So, how is your grandmother? Any better?" I asked when we were both seated in the car. Alia looked restless and fidgety. "No, no better. We called a doctor in today. They're trying to diagnose an illness but can't seem to." She was tapping her foot against the floor constantly.

"Are you okay?" I asked her.

She nodded and smiled. "Yes. Okay, well no, I'm not. I'm going to be honest. I really feel like a smoke. But," she quickly added when I sighed in exasperation, "I'm not going to have one. I've been clean for three days now. I know if I have one, I won't be able to stop." I sighed. That was a relief.

"So tell me about Shahaan's pictures. What are they like?" She asked.

"Well, I've only seen a few," I replied. "They're mostly of nature. But not the kind of nature you'd expect; no landscapes and rushing waterfalls. He captures small, unusual instances that you usually miss. Like, a close-up of an ant running on the ground during the rain." I remembered seeing that photo at the beach; it had slid out from his bag of other pictures.

Alia thought for a moment. "It would be great to have a photographer in the family. Imagine! No blurry, finger-covering-the-lens shots; nice—artistic even—family photos; and no need to hire a photographer for special events! I'm sure his family makes full use of him."

I fell silent. Shahaan had never mentioned his family. I didn't even know how many brothers and sisters he had, if any at all. On the phone, he had never said anything like, "My mother's calling me, hold a sec."

We reached the entrance of the Marriot Hotel at 6:30 p.m. Alia breezily ignored the metal detector at the entrance and walked right through it, purse and keychain still in her hand. I looked around to see if anyone had noticed. The security guard was busy opening the entrance doors. No one flinched. I did the same, quite excited when no one chased me down after the machine beeped away. "I could be carrying a gun right now," I whispered to Alia. "This place could have blown up *right now*. And there's no one who could stop it!" We laughed our way up the plush, carpeted stairs and past the heavy, branching chandelier, into the Rose Room.

There was a small cluster of people at the doorway. One security guard stood firmly at the entrance. A rifle hung casually from his shoulder. I spotted a table in the midst of the cluster of people where names on a list were being checked.

"I hope we don't need any tickets for the event," I told Alia nervously. "Shahaan didn't tell me we did."

Alia almost reeled over. She stared at me. "You have got to be kidding me. Of course we need tickets!" We eyed two middle-aged men before us, who held out two pieces of card-paper to the man at the entrance. The man at the table murmured the two men's names, slashed them off in the guest-list. They walked by airily into the room.

We were next. The man at the entrance looked at us expectantly, as if considering it rude to demand tickets off us. He was a balding man, no older than forty, wearing a waistcoat and a pair of white gloves, a neat rose peeking out of his left pocket.

"Err, tickets, madam?" he urged, holding out his gloved hand. Alia and I looked at each other and then at him. "Umm, if you'll just give me a second," I mumbled, and started fumbling in my bag for my cell phone. This had never happened to me before. I had never gate-crashed a party, turned up at a get-together uninvited, or even landed at Alia's house without telling her hours in advance. It was a habit from childhood.

On the other hand, I was also aware that my culture thrived on the *Contact System*, which, more often than not, undermined the rules. So I pulled out my phone and bit my lip agitatedly as I waited for Shahaan to pick up. He did so on the fifth ring.

"Hello, Shahaan?" I said loudly. I walked around aimlessly, trying to find good reception. "You didn't tell me we needed tickets for the exhibition!" I was trying to keep my voice low, and so my sentence came out as a muffled hiss. Shahaan told me he'd come outside right away.

Alia and I stood helplessly at the side, like mute props, watching hordes of people entering with ease. Shahaan was out in a minute, like he said. He was wearing trousers and polished, black shoes and—I was surprised to see—a blue tie. He didn't speak to us at first. He crouched over the man at the table ticking names off, and conducted a charming, urgent conversation with him, pointing to us every few seconds. "I'm sure this wouldn't have been a big deal if I dressed up more," Alia looked down at her clothes, and smirked. Before I could reply, Shahaan walked up to us and said, "Come on in. I'm so sorry." He ushered us inside the large, high-ceilinged room.

I forgot my agitation as soon as I entered the busy room. On the walls, sufficiently spaced apart, were large photos; some in small frames, others life-sized, and some that stretched from the floor to the high ceiling above. There were lush pictures of forests and waterways. There were portrait shots of people in black-and-white, sepia, and color, and then there were the more extraordinary pictures, which seemed to hold a category of their own—shots of a man's bleeding face, a snap of a monkey sitting on the back of a horse, and then a really unsettling picture of a gnarled foot.

The room was altogether dark. Spotlights shone above every photograph to illuminate them in the dim room. There were only a few other people from our age group; most looked in their fifties and sixties; art lovers, businessmen, housewives. Groups of people clustered before each photograph, whispering and nodding to each other appreciatively. "The bad part is," Shahaan said, "people don't mind coming here to appreciate the art, but you'll find few who're willing to buy it for their living room."

"I wouldn't mind buying something if I liked it," I said, observing the wall-to-wall photos.

"Oh, come on," Shahaan scoffed, smiling. "Would you rather hang a Van Gogh original in your sitting room or a picture of an old woman holding a fish taken by a Karachi local," he joked, nodding at a large, black-and-white picture of an aged woman, smiling contentedly as she held a swordfish under her arm. "People want paintings. Not photographs."

I walked a little further on, and came across a small picture, in a sepia tone, of a middle-aged woman. She was sitting on a traditional *jhoola*, a wide swing—leaning against the rail thoughtfully, with a parrot perched on her other hand. In the backdrop was a desert. The woman's hair flowed about her shoulders loosely; the *pallu* of her sari flapped in the wind. She looked like she would straighten up and fly away.

"This is beautiful," I said to Shahaan, absorbed. "I would pay for this." Shahaan didn't say anything. I looked at the white card next to the photograph. "*Ascension,*" it read. "*By Shahaan Ali.*" I whipped around and faced him. "You took this!" I exclaimed.

Shahaan shrugged, blushing. "This is a pretty old one. It was one of my first." I urged him to tell me more about it. "Well, the thought behind it is kind of whimsical, actually. This woman looks as if she's about to take off, to spread her wings and fly, but the parrot with wings stays put."

I listened and nodded. "And who's the woman in the picture?" I asked.

"That's my mother," said Shahaan.

I looked at the picture again. The woman had full lips and loose, dark hair. She portrayed the emotions required perfectly. "Oh," I said. "Random thought, but I'm just thinking how much my mother would press you to find out where your mother got her *sari* from if she were here!" We both laughed. "Let me show this to Alia." I eyed the room, searching for her. Alia had slipped off on her own, unnoticed. I finally found her before a floor-to-ceiling picture of a tulip. She was talking to someone; a man in a suit. Oh no, I thought to myself. Did these men never think twice about chatting up young girls at events? I zoomed to her rescue, ready to whisk her away from the man. But as I reached her, she was already walking away from him. She looked calm, unbothered.

"You hanging in there?" I asked her when I caught up to her.

"Yeah. Someone was trying to sell me that picture," she said. "It was forty thousand rupees! Can you believe it? And you don't have to take a long look at me to get I'm not overflowing with cash." We both burst into giggles.

When I brought Alia over and showed her Shahaan's photograph, she stood for a few moments, taking it in. "You know what this reminds me of?" she said, not taking her eyes off the picture. "My mom; this is what she would be if she hadn't given in to everyone's wishes." Before I could break the news that it was none other than Shahaan who had snapped it, she asked, "How much is this for?"

I looked at the white card. "Three thousand rupees."

"I'm going to buy it," Alia said. She looked around her. "Who do I go to?"

I stared at Alia, surprised. "Are you sure? Do you even have that much money on you?" Alia nodded. Her monthly allowance rarely spent, Alia was determined to purchase it. It made little difference, it seemed, who had taken the snapshot.

As Alia was parting with her money and having the photo wrapped, I searched the room for Shahaan. I knew he would be delighted that his picture had been sold. It hadn't even looked like many pictures had been bought that night. We were the only ones who were standing in the checkout line. I spotted Shahaan a few yards away, talking to an elder man. The man patted him on his back and smiled appreciatively. When Shahaan caught my eye, he excused himself and made his way over to us.

"Are you two ready to go?" he asked us. Alia and I nodded. Shahaan insisted dropping us home, even after I assured him that I had a car to take us back. He was having none of it. "Wait for me downstairs. I'll be down in five minutes," he said.

By the time we had sent our driver away, got into his car, and left, it was nearing nine o'clock. Alia sat in the back seat again, with her wrapped photograph by her side.

"You bought a picture, huh?" Shahaan said. "Who is the lucky artist?"

"I never found out," Alia shrugged.

"Good thinking," Shahaan said, looking at her through the rearview mirror. "If you like a painting, it doesn't matter who made it. How you felt about it is all that matters. And you look happy."

"So how many pictures of yours sold?" Alia asked casually from the back. "Or is that too personal a question?" Shahaan shook his head. "Not at all. I sold four altogether; three small frames and one large one. The painting that you liked," he turned to me, "that got sold. So, that's not so bad for a launch. I'm pretty happy."

"You should be," we both said, nodding. We were on our way to Alia's house, to drop her off first, after which I would get dropped off. I heard a comment on the weather on the radio and fumbled around with buttons, trying to turn the volume up.

"You just turned the AC off," laughed Shahaan. "It's the dial underneath that." He directed me. I found the right dial and turned the volume up. As I withdrew my hand, I accidentally opened a tiny compartment underneath the volume button. It was the slot that served as an ashtray. "Sorry," I said, trying to close it. I saw little clusters of scattered ash. It looked like mixed salt and pepper. But there was something else in there, inside a tiny packet. It was a lump of brown, like a clod of clay, wrapped in a little plastic bag and wound together with a rubber band.

The air suddenly filled with a strong, grassy odor. Next to the brown lump lay a few cigarette filters, and some tobacco. I silently stared at the items, not knowing what to say. I finally took my eyes off them to try to close the compartment. But the door didn't shut. Shahaan didn't seem to notice; his eyes were on the road. Alia heard my struggles and jumped forward from the back seat. ""Oh, for God's sake. Let me just do it." She inched her neck forward to get a good look, and froze, the way I had, when she saw what I did.

"Is everything ok?" Shahaan looked in our direction momentarily, and then gazed at what we were both looking at. "Oh," he said, dumbfounded. He paused. "Sorry, I didn't mean for you to see that. But I guess you two would eventually find out." He made no attempt to shut the compartment.

"So what is this?" I was the first to speak up. My voice trembled slightly. "Hash, marijuana?"

"Horse tranquilizer," he said gravely. Our heads spun to him in shock and then he grinned, "No, don't worry. It's just some pot."

At this point in my life, I had never had drugs. I had one or two friends who drank occasionally, and another handful that smoked. I looked at Shahaan in his smooth shirt and tie. I had never thought that he . . .

"You two look like you've been kidnapped," he said finally. He seemed carefree, as if we had just found out that he ate Cocoa Krunchies for breakfast.

"No, it's just, surprising," I said quietly, "You don't really look the type." I know I sounded foolish, not knowing what that meant.

"Does Bill Gates look like a billionaire?" he replied.

"No, I mean, I don't know. It's totally fine, really," I said, meaning it. I looked back at Alia. She had been unusually silent the whole time. I had expected her to ask him giddily, "So what does it feel like? When did you first try it?" But she was looking out the window.

"So let's change the subject," I said. "Umm, how's school?"

"I don't know," he chortled. "We're in the middle of summer holidays,"

"Right, right," I said quickly, feeling stupid. We had stopped at a traffic signal on Zamzama Street, very near to Alia's house. I heard cars honking noisily all around us. I gazed at the timer above the red traffic light. There were forty seconds left till the green light.

A young boy, no older than thirteen, suddenly crouched over the windshield. I couldn't see his face in the dark. He began cleaning the windows with a dirty rag cloth and some damp water. Shahaan sighed and gestured to the boy to stop. The boy went on, regardless, watering and swiping, watering and swiping. "Fine. Let him see if I give him any money now," Shahaan said gruffly.

On the crowded streets of Karachi, it was common to see young boys, penniless, waiting at traffic lights, and then lurching towards cars to clean windowsills while the cars were stopped at the red light. It was a way to claim money without "begging." The boys were illiterate, poor, and desperate, but also quick and nimble. They were also usually always silent. They never offered services; there was no exchange of a verbal "yes" or "no." They just cleaned. Once they were done, they stood outside one's window, small-limbed hands outstretched for money, change, or any coins one had time to give them before the light turned green and they were on their way. Their eyes were always hungry.

The boy came over to my window, as expected, to claim his money. None of us budged.

"I told him to stop," Shahaan muttered self-righteously.

But the knocks on my window grew louder and more urgent. I fished out a ten-rupee note—a tenth of a dollar—from my bag, anxious to end this awkward confrontation, and turned to the window, ready to confront a scruffy boy with large glassy eyes and an expectant face. I stumbled, however, when I found that the boy's hand was not empty. The coin fell from my hand as I looked.

I was face-to-face with a large black gun, an inch away from me, pointed at my head.

My heart and senses were numbed. I didn't even see the boy motioning, with the gun, to roll the window down. I heard Alia gasp, "Oh my God! Oh my God, oh my God," behind me. It sounded so distant, faint echoes from the bottom of a well. Shahaan eventually rolled the window down.

The boy with the gun mumbled something which I didn't hear. I could tell he was nervous because his fingers kept fumbling as if to hold a firm grip despite his sweaty palms. Shahaan had heard him. "Ok, we'll give you everything." He tried to sound calm, but his voice was shaking. He was flipping open his wallet and taking out cash. I didn't do anything at first. I just looked at Shahaan. My numbed brain then registered that I should do the same.

I fumbled in my purse, with cold hands, and took out everything; cell phone, wallet, pearl earrings that my mother had bought for me last Eid. I saw Shahaan picking at his watch and undid mine. Alia handed over her necklace, her Ipod, a few thousand rupees and a diamond-encrusted watch that I knew she had just bought in Dubai.

While this was happening, I found myself absurdly and absent-mindedly gazing at the mammoth-sized billboard above us; a woman was smiling down at me with her glass of fresh, OLPER'S MILK. *Aao kuch naya kare.* "Let's get together and start something new."

I turned to the boy to hand my things over. My eyes met with the rough gun barrel, inches away from my mouth. The boy collected the heap of the items, put the revolver inside his pocket, and walked away. I hadn't even seen his face.

All was still around me. There were several cars behind us and to our right and left. A man in the car to the left looked at us momentarily, then quickly back to the road, nervous. No sound of policemen yelling and chasing after the thief. No sirens, no women screaming from their cars or children wailing into their mother's chests. No one around us said anything.

Not one honk.

None of us spoke. All I remember hearing was the silence; like the stealthy silence that followed when a heartbeat suddenly ended. I looked at the timer over the traffic light. Now five seconds left. Everything happened in less than thirty seconds. The light flashed green and we went ahead with the sea of traffic.

It wasn't even real to me until I looked down at my empty wrist.

13

I told my mother everything; about Shahaan, the exhibition, how he had given us a ride home from the hotel. I came home on the night that it happened, and instead of running to my mother, frantic and shaken, I rushed to my bedroom. I locked the door and fell down on my bed. But I felt so scared under that cover, all alone in the silence. I knew I wouldn't be able to sleep in my own room. I crept into my mother's room at one in the morning. My father was away in China on a business trip. I felt like a thief, trying to tip-toe noiselessly to the bed, without touching anything. She hadn't heard me come in.

I crept into the bed beside her and raised the blanket over my head till it covered me entirely. The AC fuse tripped after a few minutes, and it became hot and stuffy in the room. But I refused to lift the blanket from over my head and go switch it on. I was afraid to move, to make a sound. I sweated under the suffocating blanket. But I didn't budge. I liked the darkness underneath the covers. Who said darkness was frightening? Darkness is the most comforting of all; you can't make out shapes, or figures in sheer black; they are indistinguishable. Almost . . . not there. It is in the day that the dark and menacing are in clear view; the day, where evil has nowhere to hide.

My mother found me trembling and sweaty next to her the next morning. She got worried and made me check my temperature. I was normal. But that didn't convince her. I saw her running about and rummaging through her drawers for medicine, pills, water. And then I felt I just had to tell her. I burst out crying, and between my indistinct sobs, she managed to understand what I was saying. She didn't interrupt me once as I told her about Shahaan, how he had insisted on dropping us, how quickly everything happened, between the changing of traffic lights. She saw the breathless state that I was in and tried to comfort me. "It's nothing, it's nothing," she soothed, hugging me, "only material things; cell phones, money, it doesn't matter. You are safe and that is the most important thing."

How could I explain it to her? How could she understand that it wasn't about what he had taken; it was that feeling I had at that very moment, that he would pull the gun, as if everything would just end in a second. The feeling of *waiting*, waiting for it to happen, for the trigger to go off, which was far worse than the end itself.

I wanted to call Alia and Shahaan, make sure they were all right. I was more worried about Alia. I didn't know how she had explained the story to her mom; as far as her mother knew, she was at an exhibition with me, and it was me who had dropped her back. In light of what had happened, Alia must have had no choice but to tell her the truth. I imagined the pallor that would creep into her mother's face when she realized that Alia had been lying to her; because worse than being seen with a boy was being looted with a boy. Would her pity supersede her anger?

I tried calling up Alia for the next two days. But she never came to the phone. The first time her maid told me that she was having a shower. The second time I was told she was out. I didn't buy any of it.

I hadn't heard from Shahaan either. It was as if that day had changed everything between us. At the red light we were carefree, jesting friends, and after the green light we were mute and distant, suddenly unable to recognize each other. It was like an island that had caved in from the center and dispersed into three, distinct land masses. We had just drifted away from each other.

On the third day after the incident, when I received a call on my house phone and saw Alia's number in the screen, my heart thudded with joy. I answered the phone quickly.

"Hello, is this Ayla?" It was an older woman's voice. Alia's mother.

My throat went very dry. "Yes. *Salam Alaikum*, Auntie," I answered, both disappointed that it wasn't Alia and nervous of the conversation that would ensue.

"I would like to hear, in your words—because I don't know whether what Alia is saying is true or an elaborate lie—what happened the other day." Her voice trembled, clearly trying to control the anger within.

I repeated the entire story to her, calmly.

"This has all been a horrible episode," she interrupted me. "I had never expected someone like you to lead Alia so astray. You two have been friends for so long . . . I had always trusted you, Ayla. And now you're taking my daughter behind my back, encouraging her to lie to her mother and gallivant with a boy I don't even know." She wasn't shouting; her voice was low, but indiscriminately bitter. She had never spoken to me like this before. Nasreen Aunty had only addressed me with the most courtesy and kindness whenever I had come over. When she didn't allow Alia to go out, it was often me who managed to cajole her out of her decision. What was happening?

I remained silent while she went on about how disappointed she was in me; after she was through, she asked to speak to my mother. I called Ma and handed her the phone, saying nothing. I felt numb and unfeeling. Perhaps I should have expected this to happen. Sooner or later . . . it had to happen. I exited the room while they spoke; the last thing I wanted was to see the look of disappointment on my mother's face when she found out. She hadn't been pleased about Shahaan at all. But I hadn't told her that Alia had lied to her mother in order to come out with us. It wasn't as if I was trying to hide anything; I just thought it was unnecessary to bring up the trivial details at a time like this.

My mother did not think it was a trivial detail. She questioned me after she finished speaking with Nasreen Aunty. This time, she thoroughly interrogated me, asking for every single detail; the circumstances and the background. After hearing me out, she said that it wouldn't be wise of me to meet Alia at this time. Nasreen Aunty was taking Alia to their farmhouse in Malir in two weeks. She thought that she needed a long break; a chance to straighten herself out. Inside however, I knew it was nothing more than a ploy to get her away from me.

With nothing to do now, I tried to busy myself with different things. I remember reading until very late at night, often even after I heard birds chirping outside. I didn't have a very large book collection, but I didn't mind re-reading what I did have. Often, I'd look outside my window and see the first trace of morning while I was flipping through pages.

I thought back to the days when school was open; when Alia and I could meet first thing in the morning and relay stories of what we had done over the weekend, and groan about how much homework we had to complete. We only had world history together, and so that class became a refuge for us.

I thought back to the time that I had teased Alia endlessly about her red organizer. On our first day of school that year, Alia had come to class with a bag more full than expected. From it she had unleashed a jumbo, album-sized red organizer. She had made a resolution to be more organized that year. The album, or "plan-book" as she liked to call it, was as intricate and detailed as a telephone directory. There were so many different categories and time-slots, and fancy names for words like "date-book" and "events." She used that diary *incessantly* for a month. She wrote down all her class notes in it (although I don't know where she found the space on those cramped pages), she scrawled reminder notes on almost every page; she even made a special section for TV schedules. The planner was her bible; over time it became something of a sacred source of knowledge. If you wanted to know which episode of *American Idol* was next showing, it was in the planner. You wanted the different dates of the reigns of each of the Mogul rulers? It was in that planner. Wanted the number of that Italian restaurant which served the best fillet-o-fish in town? Yes, the planner.

And finally, like all people do of their hobbies, like clerks do of their jobs, like accountants do of paychecks, and refuse collectors do of refuse, Alia got sick of it. The planner was taking over her life. Now every time she thought of taking a shower or going to bed, she felt she couldn't do so without consulting the planner. She couldn't cope with the rigid schedule set down by it; over time she grew almost afraid to look at it, to know what all she hadn't done, what she had put off, or failed to do. Finally, she conceded bitterly, "My parents are enough to remind me what a loafer I am; I don't need a planner to do it." So that was the end of the organizer. I actually felt sad when I saw Alia discard it in her top-hand, hard-to-reach shelf. "I'm going to throw some philosophical load at you, as you're prone to do with me at times like these," I said to her, diving at the opportunity. "If your life is already planned," I looked heavenward, "then the only thing you have the power to do is . . . live it."

I thought back to those days while I lay awake at night, in my dark room. I wondered how long Alia's mother would keep her from the city. I wanted desperately to talk to her, and to hear her say that her mother's opinion of me would never change anything. Because deep inside, I was fearful that it wasn't so.

Saturday arrived rather quickly and I had a yoga class to go to. I was looking much more forward to meeting Tanzeela now that I had very few familiar people in my life. Surprisingly, she arrived at Ghazal's house before I did. There wasn't enough space up in front so I had to sit at the back of the room, and hope that she had seen me. After the class was over, we met at the same spot by the speakers to drink water. "I have good news," Tanzeela said, tilting her head back to take a swig. "My car won't be picking me up until a little later. So we can get some coffee next door!" She looked at me for my response.

"That's great." I couldn't have hoped for anything better.

When we entered the same café and took our seats, she began, "I felt really bad the other day, for dashing out of here like that." I told her it wasn't a problem. She seemed to notice my discontented mood. "Are you all right?" she asked, clasping both her hands together and placing them underneath her chin.

I didn't wave my feelings away and shrug, saying "It's nothing." I hadn't spoken to anyone about how I had felt after the episode on Tuesday. My mother knew the details of what had happened but there was no one I could speak to, not even Alia, about how I *really* felt. I needed to talk to someone.

I told Tanzeela everything. Her large, black pupils widened in shock when she heard how we had been robbed. I told her how hard it was, not being able to speak to Alia after the episode, being scolded by Alia's mother like I was some kind of delinquent, and then, on top of everything else, not hearing a trace of Shahaan either. It was as if I had verbal hemophilia; my words came pouring out uncontrollably, and continuously, with little resistance.

"You're right to feel horrible," Tanzeela nodded. "The shock of everything that happened, and then this sudden loneliness after. You and Alia must be very close." She smiled. I nodded to her. "You know, I had a best friend in school as well," Tanzeela said, looking distant. "And that wasn't very long ago! Her name was Sabeen. We were childhood friends, you know. Inseparable."

"So, where is she now?" I asked. Tanzeela shrugged, and laughed. It was a sad laugh. "I don't know. Things just changed after I told her I was getting married. She couldn't bear to talk to me after that. She said it made her sad." She said the last sentence with clear sarcasm.

"Oh." I suddenly felt foolish saying what I had said. Alia and I hadn't spoken for a few days and I was getting teary about it. I couldn't imagine what Tanzeela must have gone through. To have lost her childhood friend, her only confidante at a time when she was going through a stage as tumultuous as that . . . it was frightening. But I knew the last thing she wanted was for me to dole out the pity card.

"I'll be honest," I said. "I myself can't imagine what it would be like to be married . . . and now, I, I can't even comprehend it. Is it hard?"

Tanzeela circled her finger around the rim of her empty glass. "Yes. But it's not the maintenance of the marriage itself that I find hard. It's just . . . adjusting to a new house with new people. You start to realize you have duties to fulfill, and it's not all about you. I have no time to myself anymore."

I looked at her, confused. "What kind of duties do you mean? Housework?" It didn't seem to make sense. I had been to the house; there were enough maids and cleaners to cater to their needs.

"No," she replied, absent-mindedly scratching the side of her neck. "Not the housework itself. But the supervision of all the cooks and maids is stressful enough. I don't do the actual cooking but I have to tell them *what* to cook, how to cook it. And telling isn't enough. You have to stand there by their side, and hold their hand, literally." She sighed. "And then there's the gardener to direct, the grocery-shopping . . . it all becomes so exhausting." She clutched the sides of her temples with each hand and closed her eyes.

I felt a little lost. Maybe I was wrong about her; maybe she really wasn't being abused. Perhaps she was just so wrecked with pressure that she was unable to give enough time to herself. But then, why did she seem so sad? It had to be more than just house work . . . what else could explain that unmistakable, woeful look in her eyes, as if she had been robbed and looted even worse than I had?

"So what do you like to do when you *do* get time off?" I asked. I felt my coffee get cold between my hands. The froth was beginning to disappear, and little streaks of milky white appeared in its place, swirling around the center like a spinning vortex.

"I usually sleep, or watch TV. But when I get the whole day free— when the cooks are on leave—I like to sit down and make pottery."

I raised my eyebrows. "Pottery? That's interesting."

She smiled slightly. "Yes. I don't even mind getting my hands dirty for it. It's such a mystifying art . . . made to perfection . . . the smoothness of the edges, the symmetry and perfect alignment of the mold . . . every clay pot is a testament to the beauty of mathematics." She seemed to daze off, dreamily. "Do I sound mad?" She laughed.

I shook my head. I told her that I held passion for art as well, something I hadn't mentioned before. "I think that's the magic of the word *art*," I said, "it doesn't need to be a drawing on paper. It's so many, many different things."

By the time we finished and paid the check, it was already 7:30 p.m. It had begun raining heavily outside. Trees shook and swayed in the fierce wind, like dancing flames on the wick of a candle, to and fro, to and fro. Shopkeepers frantically began closing their shops down, yelling to others to do the same. Cars screeched out of the driveways, and women hurried along down the roads, wrapping their *dupattas* around them to protect themselves from the rain. Everyone wanted to get home.

"Well, I'll see you next week, then," Tanzeela said. She scanned the road until she spotted her car. I nodded in agreement. I started off in the direction of my car, when I saw a dark figure in the misty light approaching me. I tried to make out the figure, looking for familiarity. The lights above me flickered noisily and then suddenly went off. It was pitch dark. I felt slightly scared, standing in the middle of that noisy street. Flashes of the past week started twitching in my mind, like the flickering lights. I was going to be shot. I knew it. I had escaped the first time but it wouldn't happen again. I turned my back on the dark figure and walked hurriedly. I didn't know where I was going, but I wanted to escape from it, whoever it was.

"Wait!" called a voice behind me. "Don't run away. It's me." I recognized that voice. I stopped and turned. The light suddenly flickered back on. The dark figure was Shahaan. I sighed heavily.

"What's wrong?" he said, laughing. "Did you think I was going to mug you?"

My heartbeat slowed down to normal. The fear that had consumed me had released its firm grip and was slowly walking away. I was relieved. "What are you doing here?" I asked him.

He shrugged. "Your phone number got taken away with my phone. And I don't remember it. Then I recalled you telling me about your yoga classes. It was a little hard to find," he looked around the dim, gray alley and smirked, "you had only told me it was on Twenty-sixth Street. But I did a bit of asking around and . . ."

"No, you don't understand," I said. "I meant, *why* are you here?" We were standing on the road now, unprotected. Raindrops were creeping down my neck and into my scalp. Shahaan was already soaking wet.

"I can't talk to you like this," he said. He nodded his head toward his car and motioned to me. "Give me five minutes." I relented and walked with him toward his car. When we were inside, he handed me a handful of Kleenex. I wiped my face and neck, and waited for him to say something. "I wanted to know how you were doing," he started. "I haven't spoken to either of you after the . . . incident." I felt a vein in my head throb slightly. That's why he had come all the way here? To ask me how I was feeling?

"I'm doing much better," I told him. "I don't know about Alia." I told him what had happened with her mother, how she was going to be leaving in a week for Malir. Shahaan looked very surprised, and, it seemed, sad for me. He suddenly went quiet.

"And how has it been for you?" I asked him. "You seem to be thriving." We both giggled.

"I should tell you something." He said, looking down at his hands, resting on his lap. He then looked up at me. "My father . . . he's a cobbler. He fixes shoes." I stared at him, silent. I didn't understand. Shahaan looked ahead now. "It wasn't quite as bad as that, even. He was jobless; his father hadn't sent him to school because they didn't have any money. So at the age of twenty-three, my father started off mending buckles for friends. He realized he was pretty good at it. He opened a tiny shop in Sadder. It got off to a slow start but then it became quite popular. He hired a few workers and moved the shop to Tariq Road. Customers started pouring in. That's when he met my mother. She was a customer." He paused. "She was a receptionist at a local estate agent's office; not extremely well-off, but, in a comfortable position. They fell for each other. She was willing to leave her family behind for him, run away and get married. He promised that he would learn English, get a good job, and make himself worthy of her family. One night, he closed the shop extra early, and took her out of the city with him on his motorcycle. They got married. They actually thought they were quite happy, that it would last.

"But he never got a job. She tried to teach him English, but he was impatient. He hated the language, and became more and more defensive. She started missing her family. It would never have worked out. They separated after a year of marriage, and then got divorced three months after. My father went back to his craft, opening up a shop in Tariq Road. My mother went back to her family. That's when she realized that she was pregnant. Her parents refused to let her go back to him, child or no child. They wanted her to forget the whole episode; pretend as if it had never happened. My grandmother even threatened to abandon my mother if she told me who my real father was. So she didn't. Not until both her parents passed away. I was twelve then. Now my mother and I live alone, in a small apartment, with an old maid who visits every week. My mother found a job as a flight attendant. She's not around a whole lot of the time. When I came back home that night, she was away in Zurich."

My insides churned in anguish. I pictured Shahaan coming back home after the incident, stirred and shaken, and opening the door to an empty, dark house with no one, nowhere to go to but bed, no one and nothing to cry on but his own shoulder.

"H-have you ever seen him?" I asked. He gave me a blank look. "Your father." My throat was feeling dry, scratchy, as if I had swallowed a cup of flour.

He shook his head slowly. "Only in pictures." There was silence. "It's all good," he grinned, loosely and easily. "Yeah, it was kind of hard coping with it on my own, but that's how it's always been for me, I guess. Hey, the good thing is, I don't need to explain a missing cell phone and watch to anyone," he laughed to himself. But the laugh was hollow, and seemed affected.

"Are you sure you're fine?" I asked him. He nodded too quickly. "I don't believe you," I said abruptly. "But I'll wait till you're ready." He looked up and gazed at me, half-smiling. I smiled back. "Yup, I'm borrowing a page from your book."

"Yeah, clever of you," he nodded. "So . . . are you ever going to show me a painting of yours?" He turned to me.

I swallowed and nodded. "When it's complete." He asked me what I was working on now but I told him he would have to wait; I wasn't giving any hints.

"You know, I've always wondered why you're so secretive about your art," he said. "Do all experts do that?"

"I do it because I like a genuine reaction," I answered. "I never ask people what they think of my work when I show it to them. I can just feel their response from that initial expression. And if they don't have any pre-warning of what my work will look like, the more accurate the reaction."

Shahaan laughed and shook his head. "You artists." There was silence for a while.

I stared at the raindrops running down his windshield; blurring our view. I could only make out indistinct shapes through the dripping window. Colors were hazy, and seemed to dissolve into one another. "Gosh, is this what it's like to be blind?" I thought out aloud, touching the window, trying to see through it.

Shahaan turned to the soaking window and grinned. "No, this is what it's like to have perfectly good vision."

"What do you mean?" I asked him.

"We only see partially. Don't you think?"

I looked in the opposite direction and laughed. "You know, you really are an enigma."

"Why?"

"You never act this way in front of Alia."

"What do you mean?"

"I mean, you're like a different person when we're all together. You're just like any other boy; no better, no worse. But when we're alone, your philosophical streak comes out; it's all poetry and heavy words. Is this your true side? Or is that your original side—the one you show when you're around Alia? I just can't figure you out." I don't know where this sudden eruption had come from. It had never even—consciously—bothered me before.

"I . . . I'm sure this is my real side," he looked uncertain, confused. "I don't know how to answer that. I consider you closer than Alia, maybe that's why I haven't been able to open up to her as much. But my real side . . . I don't understand what you mean by that. You know, you act differently when you're around your family, differently even towards each of your friends. You do it unconsciously. Everyone does. We all show different shades of our personality to everyone, like, you know, different clips from a slideshow . . . you know that, don't you? So what would you do if I asked you, Ayla, out of all the different sides that you present to the world, what is your real side? I'm sure your answer to me would be the one I have for you: I don't know."

I fell silent. It was pouring now, faster and with greater force. Half an hour had gone by. I had switched my new phone on silent mode while I was at Ghazal's, and had forgotten to resume it to normal. My mother was probably ringing me endlessly, anxious that the rain had done something to me. I knew she was calling my chauffeur as well. He must have told her that I was nowhere in sight. Of course he speculated about whether I was kidnapped but dared not suggest it to my mother. She was yelling at him for not being more observant; worrying and calling me again and again, hoping with every ring that I'd pick up this time. I felt at peace. No one could see me behind the cloudy, dripping window.

No one could shoot me.

"Hey, why don't we go inside the café?" I asked. "Better to just sit there for a few minutes than out here in the rain?" Shahaan shrugged, and we both walked back inside the café where I had been with Tanzeela half an hour ago. We took the same table as I had been in earlier. My coffee mug was still sitting there, collecting brown foam at the base.

Shahaan turned towards the large plasma screen at the café, and then motioned to the waiter. "*Bhai*, brother, you think you could switch the channel to Star Sports? There's a big cricket match on today. Pakistan versus the Netherlands."

"So what did it feel like," I asked Shahaan, breaking the silence. "When you tried it for the first time?" I looked at his nonplussed expression and elaborated, "Marijuana. How did it feel?"

Shahaan fumbled in his seat, distracted. "That referee needs to get kicked out." He clucked his tongue at the TV screen. "Batsman was totally in the clear. Our team's a goner." He cleared his throat and turned to me, "Why do you want to know what it felt like?"

"Did it feel like you had jumped off a waterfall?" My voice had almost shrunk to a whisper, and my tone had come out mocking, almost sardonic. I hadn't meant for it to.

"No," he answered, surprising me. "I felt like I had just seen God."

"What did He look like?" I asked.

"How do I know, I was high!" He looked at my serious expression and burst out laughing. "But seriously," he said, once his chuckle subsided to near-silence, "I did feel like I saw God. I don't remember what He looked like. Maybe that's why I like taking pot more and more; it brings me to God each time."

"You think it might be the other way round?" I asked. "That maybe your lack of faith has led to your habit? Everyone needs to be grounded, to have some sort of stability. Faith provides that for many people. It gives you purpose. Even if you're not a keen follower."

Shahaan paused for a moment and then laughed, looking at me, eyebrows raised. "Lack of faith?" he jeered. "I think my problem is that I have *too* much faith. So much faith that I'm unable to invest it in one single God!" He shrank down in his seat.

Seconds ticked away. All of a sudden, Shahaan and a number of other young men in the café jumped from their seats. "Sixer!!! That's what I'm talking about!" Shahaan pumped his fist in the air. There was a general "dude" feeling in the café now, all the guys around Shahaan's age high-fiving one another and praising Shahid Afridi's batting skills. I looked at the television and sure enough, Shahid Afridi—the batsman—was raising his bat in the air with both hands, his heavy helmet rattling, jubilantly leading our team to its victory.

My father always joked that cricket bought people in this country together, even if we were at each other's throats. The upper class and the poor, the extreme and the modern—they all came together when it came to cricket. Fights were suspended. Sunnis and Shias embraced each other when a batsman scored six runs. Cricket suspended lines that separated us. Made us rally around something that had nothing to with politics, or religion. Here I was, a Sunni who belonged to the upper elite class, and I could have been sitting next to Shias, next to workers and cobblers and tailors of different classes and backgrounds. But none of those class or religious lines mattered when we all shouted at the screen in excitement.

A boy about sixteen years old then came to our table and shook hands with Shahaan. His hair was short and clipped, and he wore a lot of denim. Denim jacket, denim jeans. A cloud of imperceptible dark-wash Levis blue. "*Kya haal hai, bhai?*" "How are you, brother?" He had a strong voice, deep.

"Good. *Acha* game *chal raha hai.* Good game. Let's hope we win, man. We've got to recover against our defeat with India."

"That's Rehaan. A boy who goes to my school." Shahaan told me when the denim-boy walked away. "Pretty happening café here, wish you told me about it sooner!" He looked around, delivering an expression of firm approval at the crowded tables, the energetic chit-chatter of high-schoolers, people like us who were seeking refuge in this stirring, warm and bustling café during the rain.

When the air had calmed down momentarily, I said, "I just thought you would want to know. Alia bought your photograph at the exhibition."

"Wow, that's really cool. I had no idea." He seemed distracted, though. "So anyway, I was just wondering . . . you still haven't told me . . . why does Alia call you piggy?"

"It's nothing, really. It's not a big secret. The way you're saying it, it's like it was the Da Vinci code," I chuckled. "I was on summer vacation in Italy one year, and unknowingly ate pork. Growing up, my mother always told me pork was *haram*, forbidden. To convince me, she said that pork was the meat of the devil, and if I ate it, I would grow devil wings. Yeah, I know. I actually believed it. You'll be amazed at the things kids will believe when adults say it to them with a straight face. But anyway, so I tried some pepperoni while in Italy, and had no idea it was pork. And I loved it. I ate it again and again, thinking that 'bacon' was just a fancy word for 'chicken sausage.' Almost every night during that Italy trip, I'd wait for my family to go to sleep in the hotel, then run downstairs to the food and deli market and buy something called 'bacon jerky.' It's this dried looking bacon you get in packets. You should try it sometime."

"That's pretty hilarious."

"So I finally came back to Pakistan—vacation over, and spoke to Alia over the phone. I told her the Italian food I ate was amazing; that she better try the *bruschetta* and the bacon. And she stopped me right there. And told me I'd been eating pig the whole summer. I don't know what it was. It was psychological. I felt like I'd literally eaten devil's meat. I mean, I was ten, this was the scariest thing I'd been told my whole life! So I threw up, right there, while I was on the phone with Alia. All over my mom's cream-colored carpet. It was a bad day. Since then, I feel squeamish every time I looked at pepperoni. Alia thought it was hilarious. So she began calling me 'piggy.' Gripping story, right?" I smiled, and Shahaan laughed. It was a deep laugh, one that resounded all over his body. His shoulders shook a little and his long hair flopped over his face. I looked at him for a second and thought to myself how great it was to see him smile and laugh like this after so long. After weeks of not talking. And being scared. Everything felt calm. And just right.

But that calm was momentary. Because the next second, and before we had even touched our waiting coffee, a waiter—a dark-skinned, heavy man—burst out of the kitchen, yelling, his eyes red and popping from his skull. "Benazir Bhutto killed! Benazir Bhutto killed!"

The TV screen in the café then flickered. The channel, which had panned to Pakistani cricket captain Inzamam-ul-Haq's sweat-soaked, gleaming face, talking about Netherland's defeat against Pakistan and how Pakistan was gearing up for the next cricket match, suddenly went blank.

Everyone in the café stopped talking. The waiter was on his knees now, pulling at his hair and wailing in short, sudden gasps.

The blank TV suddenly started blinking. Uncontrollably. We all stared.

BENAZIR BHUTTO, PRESIDENTIAL CANDIDATE, ASSAS-SINATED IN RAWALPINDI DURING ELECTION RALLY.

A newscaster's face appeared, red, troubled. BOMB BLAST EXPLOSION. AL-QAEDA SUICIDE BOMBER RESPONSIBLE. ASSASSINATION PLANNED BY MUSTAFA AL-YAZID.

Names were now flashing on the newscast. Bits of information at racing speed, as if being flung in the viewer's face mockingly. As if to say, *This has happened. This is real. You deal with this now.*

I momentarily wondered how many of the world's tragedies—nat-ural calamities, politician's assassinations, homicides, and deaths—had begun with broadcasts like this—with sudden blank TV screens in front of viewers. And then flickers. Interruptions of people watching the local news, or sitting with their children to see Nickelodeon spe-cials on Sunday. One second you were lounging on the couch thinking about what kind of waffles to eat with your breakfast, or who would win the cricket world cup, and the next you were confronted with news that there was a tsunami in East Asia. You then panic with the realization that this is isn't just about you—there is a world outside this living room and your friends and the things you call possessions, and your false sense of safety in your living room shrinks.

And then I wondered what it was like for the news reporters actually conveying this news. Coming to work expectantly and sitting in their makeup chairs and being told in an industrious voice by a TV producer, *Change of plans from that thing you were going to report about the community village fair—the Prime Minister has just died—you're up on the air to talk about it in five. Let's do a makeup change first. This is serious business. Just remember—solemn voice!*

I looked at the news reporter on this screen. He was sweating. His black-rimmed glasses slid down his nose as he bleated out the Al-Qaeda commander's seething words. "Al-Qaeda has claimed responsibility for the attack. Al-Yazid, the mastermind behind the attack, has stated, *We terminated the most precious American asset which vowed to defeat the mujahedeen—our freedom fighters.*"

I looked around me. A girl on the table next to us was holding her hair, crying. The boy in the denim jeans and jacket—Rehan—who a second earlier had taken off his denim jacket and swung it around his head in joy,—was out of his seat, wide-eyed, gaping. He walked up to Shahaan and said, "Brother. We have to get out of here now. Riots are going to begin. This city is going to be in flames."

In flames. What did that mean? I looked at Shahaan but he was already somewhere else, his eyes blank.

All of a sudden, the lights in the café went out. The waiters now were yelling to the customers in the darkness. "Please leave, we are now closed! Go home! Leave!" We left our plates and coffee and ran outside the building. I heard yelling, howling. There were people lined up on the road now, people wailing, loudly. People running in groups, trying to get quickly into cars. A bus pulled up in front of us, teeming with people. I saw a group of men throw themselves on the side of the bus, climbing up to the top and yelling for the bus to move, to drive away.

"Come with me, now," Shahaan said to me, moving me in the direction of his car. "You, too, Rehan. We have to stick together."

"Wait, I need to find my car. My driver is there. I don't know if he's still here. I can't just leave with you." I looked to the spot where my car had stood, and found it was still standing there. But my chauffeur was nowhere to be seen.

"Your driver has probably run away, panicked," Shahaan hissed. "Come with me now, we need to go somewhere safe." With that, he pulled my hand and we moved quickly toward his car. And we walked in the dark, the rain pushing against us violently.

The road in front of me was black with rain and despair. It was glaring dark; not even a street light was on. Restaurants that were open and playing loud music had now closed and shops had firmly locked their shutters. Fireflies and mosquitoes hovered around the headlights of the remaining cars. Wailings, rising in the cold, raining wind, went unhindered.

As we got into the car, strangers struggled to get in with us. They pressed their wet palms against our window shield and clawed on the hood of the car. The inside of the car was rumbling with the noise of this impact. Shahaan hurriedly started the ignition and muttered, "Bloody hell, it's going to be impossible to get out of here."

"What is going on? Why is everyone rushing to leave like this?" I asked him, looking at crying children holding on to their mothers as they walked around stricken and desperate.

"Because it's going to get violent. Benazir Bhutto's political party had many campaign supporters. Regular, working class people. They are angry. And aggrieved. And they sure as hell hate her political rival, our President—Musharraff. These people want revenge and they don't give a shit if people get hurt." Shahaan honked loudly at the car in front of him. "They are going to come to the streets. Probably armed. We need to get out of this traffic jam. We have to."

I started sobbing now. Tears fell easily from my eyes. My family had always been pro-Musharraff. We had voted for the President—Bhutto's opponent—and supported him for years now. At the same time, my family and I always looked up to Benazir Bhutto. She was politically liberal and had led our country in the nineties, a time when the country had sore relations with India and needed strong leadership. She had now returned to Pakistan after years of self-imposed exile to lead the country to a better future—to a future with a chance of democracy. My family supported her ideals—even if we didn't necessarily support her party. But Bhutto couldn't even make it past elections. Not in this country. Not in a country where a simple election couldn't go unhindered without mob violence.

In the dark I saw men with heavy wooden clubs and flashlights slowly infiltrating the streets. As the lights flickered on their faces, I saw they had long beards. They heard us honk. One of the men—a tall man, soaking wet and gripping his black beard feverishly, pointed at our car and said something non-distinct to the group of men. Within seconds, five of them descended on our car. Their expressions were cold, empty.

"They're coming towards us, Shahaan." I held my breath, my heart sinking. But surprisingly, the mob came toward us and then passed our car, aiming for the car next to us. I turned left and saw a blue Honda with a middle-aged man on the driver's seat. His mouth was open in fear. He honked loudly, but there was no point. One of the men in the mob, a tall wiry man with a black beard, unblinkingly took a jack and speared it through the driver's window. Glass shattered noisily. "*Jeay* Bhutto!" He heaved. *Long live Bhutto.* The woman in the passenger's seat was crying loudly and pressing a bundle—a baby to her chest. More glass shattered. I shut my eyes and felt heavy tears in my lids.

"Please don't hurt us. For the sake of God, please don't hurt us." The man was wailing next to us.

The men didn't care. They were chanting loudly now. "*Jeeeay Shaheed* Bhutto!" "Long live the martyr!" Thumping their fists and clubs against the car doors. I couldn't make myself look anymore.

Shahaan was gritting his teeth at the car in front of us. "Come on, just fucking move, just fucking move!"

I then felt a loud THUMP against the window and knew that it was our turn. I looked right, and found myself facing the man with the black club through the window. He had a large cleft on his lip, and was yelling something I couldn't understand. Angry, meaningless words. His friends were slapping our windows now, chanting. Wailing. Cursing. The man aimed his club at us and pounded on the top of the car. The car shook momentarily, and I felt the onslaught of more. Just as he took aim again, Shahaan pressed the gas and the traffic suddenly—magically—moved, and we sped out and away from the mob. I looked behind me and saw the bearded group of men spit on the ground, enraged that we got away, and look around for more cars to vandalize, to smash and break.

We drove and drove and drove. Rehan suddenly whispered, "Oh my God," and I turned to my right. Smoke from outside drifted into our car, and made us choke on our own coughs. On the side of the street, a slew of cars were engulfed in flames.

A canister of gasoline was thrown carelessly at the foot of one of the burning cars, evidence that the cars were torched by aggrieved, violent men. The flames danced weakly in the rain, sending cinders and smoke hurling in the air. A billboard sat high above the flaming cars. I looked at Benazir Bhutto's face, smiling, benevolent. The slogan: "Democracy is the best revenge."

14

Personal Statement Essay—Cornell University
Early Decision Application
Ayla Sattar
9 October 2007

"Spark"

Somewhere far off, in a barren land twenty thousand miles away, a flash of lightning sounds. Silence. A slight twitch. Two creatures meet and regard each other with hostility. One is suspicious of the other. The other doesn't recognize the first. They eventually join hands. A spark. The first creature invites many from his tribe, just like him. The second only brings along a few others. They collide. A flicker. They bask in the water. Drip, drip. Friction. And then a mighty explosion.

A cell is born.

But why does this matter to me? I've never been wholly interested in molecular science. But biology is necessary. It gives whole shapes to abstract thoughts. When I sit tapping my pencil against my desk, wondering why Pakistan, the country I was born in, hasn't embraced democracy, I don't need to look far beyond. It is rather simple. On one side stands democracy, a grainy enzyme, and on the other stands autocracy, its target, both separated by a partial barrier. A membrane, if you will. One tries, but can't penetrate all the way to the other side. A molecule cannot enter if it is too large. Is democracy too overwhelming, too great an ideal? Perhaps. In my country we have neither the will, nor the courage to absorb it, much as we need it. Nature has its way.

English literature is what I truly love. But it seems to do the opposite of what biology does; biology gives a context and shape for my thoughts; literature lets them scatter freely and far into the wild.

"What was the use of poets?" they say. "All poets do is dream." My country began as a dream. The vision of a mere poet, Allama Iqbal, who dreamt of a separate homeland for our people after years of colonialism.

I don't read the verses of Shelley and Keats for the satisfaction they give me. I see a clear message, a truth lurking under imagery of rushing waterfalls and purple skies. It just takes a little time to find out what is.

Whitman cried, "I sing the song of pleasure and pain." Dissect it. Take it apart. Now examine under slide. What was Whitman saying? That pleasure and pain are opposing, but necessary. There is beauty in the opposites. Wasn't I surrounded by contradiction? Extremism conflicted with moderation. Feudalism verses capitalism. Militants taking up arms against government. Bomb blast at female politician's return home.

Poets only provide questions, never answers. And they find beauty in everything, don't they? They see pearls of white in salty tears. Maybe they will see falling embers in the tears my country shed for their loved ones who died in the suicide bomb last week. Maybe they will describe people's opposition to martial law in neat couplets.

People say my combination of subjects is odd. But I can't resist them. Combined, they give me a unique perspective of my world, a perspective that I know no one else can have. I want to bring democracy to my country, go against the diffusion gradient, against nature if I have to. I may never truly know the reason behind conflict. But there aren't always answers. Sometimes you just need to use your imagination. After all, even the mightiest world disaster did once begin as a cell in some barren land, far, far away . . .

~

School was shut for five days following the attack. President Musharraf declared a three-day period of mourning. I sat in my room, distractedly studying. No word from Shahaan. No word from Alia.

The TV was on most of the day when I returned home. I saw images of the streets in Rawalpindi, where Benazir Bhutto had been killed. She had been on a campaign rally. She was shot in the neck and the chest as she stood on the sunroof vehicle to greet supporters while leaving the rally. The bomber then blew himself up, witnesses said. Blood smeared the curbs of street corners. People were yelling for ambulances. Twenty people were killed in the suicide bomb attack.

It's just a specimen, I muttered to myself, my eyes shut.

If you want to be a surgeon, you have to stand the sight of blood. There was no other way about it.

I had looked at the breezy doctors in their lab coats at the hospitals, their names inscribed in capital letters on breast pockets, and wondered to myself, how did they manage to do that? Did they pretend that the blood was red paint, dye? You had to learn how to slice through muscle and tendon skillfully, like a craftsman, without dismembering any other part of the system. I had jokingly thought to myself that surgeons must be able to cut their meat at the table splendidly well.

And then I finally saw a surgeon at work. He was my father's friend. He had allowed me to observe one of his bigger surgeries at the local hospital. I remember seeing many instruments: scalpel, razor blade, tweezers, hack-saw. They were gleaming and spotless, sparkling trophies assembled together.

The patient had rickets. He was a young boy, maybe even my age. He lay unconscious on the surgical table, tubes going in and out of him, everywhere. One tube to desensitize him. One to revive him. One to check that he was still there.

"You know, you must think this gruesome; pulling people apart and inserting things into them," said the doctor. He looked at me, and I could sense him smiling underneath the surgical mask. "But this is what people—what we all—do day in and day out. We see a problem. We take it apart, dissect it. We find the weak link, the root cause of the disaster. And then we get rid of it. You might do this problem solving a lot more often than you think you do." He chuckled.

I nodded and answered, "Yes. Except there usually isn't blood involved."

The surgeon raised his eyebrows and replied, "True. But name me one problem that isn't messy."

The surgeon then wasted no time; scalpel in hand, he dove into flesh, revealing the hidden, the parts that we were all ashamed off. I observed the epidermal layer, the pale and smooth muscle, giving way to subcutaneous fat layers, blood, fluid, and then finally, bone. "You have to tell yourself during the surgery," he said, *"It's not a human, it's a specimen."* I tried to slow down my quickening heart. I had to get used to the sight of blood. I had to concentrate. "And here is the part of the femur that we need to fix," said the surgeon, indicating the bone. Yes, the femur. It was bent in one position. It needed to be put back in place; straightened by inserting a metal rod into the bone . . .

I couldn't help it. I looked at the unconscious boy's face. Patient X. He was lying down on his side, facing me. His eyelids were half-open, and a tear had settled in the inner corner of his eye.

He knew what was happening.

I lifted the surgical mask off my face, placed it on the side table, and walked out of the room. I wasn't strong enough. I didn't know if anyone had noticed me leave, but no one stopped me, and no one came after me. Maybe they expected it. They knew it was my first time. "Let her go," the surgeon must have said to his assistants. "She'll come back once she's better." But I didn't go back. I couldn't.

It's not a human, it's a specimen. It's not a human, it's a specimen.

Little did I know how much I had to cajole myself with that phrase during the week that would follow the suicide bomb attack.

When we finally returned to school, we were instructed to go to biology lab and undertake our first dissection.

I stared, glassy-eyed at the heart that faced me in biology class. I had forceps in my right hand and a sharp pair of tweezers in my left. It was my first, hands-on dissection. We had hung outside the labs before class, pushing each other and jeering, "You can't take it."

I had expected the specimen to be a frog; bisected into two, and stitched down to the tray on all four corners, as if crucified. Others vouched that it would be a kidney; apparently that was far easier to slice. Finally, we went in to the labs, single file. The air smelled *chemical*. We lined up to use hand sanitizer.

I wished that they had given us gloves.

No one had thought that it would be a heart. It just felt much too soon for that. For the first few seconds, we sat, wide-eyed, in front of our specimens, trying to figure out what it was. It was just a lump of murky brown. If someone had put it in a wine glass, smeared some chocolate syrup over it, and laid it down before me, I would have thought it was custard. I had thought it was a kidney at first; small, plush, covered in lubricating fluid. But then my eye caught the thick, muscular tube running out from the top right-hand of the organ; it was the unmistakable aorta.

I picked up the scissor and tweezers. Right, I told myself. Let's cut this up nice and quick. Foolishly, I had thought that I could perform the entire dissection without getting my hands dirty. I held the forceps firmly in place and cut the muscular wall open. Ah, things were beginning to make sense now. There was the right atrium—it seemed so much smaller than in the book—and here was the tricuspid valve, held in place by the unmistakable *chordae tendinae*, thin and firm, like the strings on a harp. For a few seconds it had stopped becoming a heart to me, and more a cluster of terms and tissues. I looked up for a moment. There were thirty-two students in the lab. Sixty-four hearts in the room, altogether. Half had had their rhythm abruptly cut short. Half were beating much faster than usual.

I looked down at the specimen, and suddenly felt it quiver in my hands. Something twitched for a split second. Alarmed, I paused and looked at it closely. When the heart had been ripped out from the goat, or sheep, or whatever it was, there was still blood in it, ready to be pumped off. That blood had been released now, onto the metal tray underneath, now with nowhere to go, as if it had boarded an airplane only to realize that there was no destination. The organ was sitting in a pool of plasma—waiting for the next flight? The composure with which I had performed the necessary dissection had all but vanished.

There was blood in my hands.

I tried to pry open the pulmonary artery with the scalpel, and my fingers shook. I withheld too quickly and the scalpel cut through my finger. I put the scalpel down and watched it silently. There was a brief pause, after which my blood seeped out; transparent, like red paint that had been mixed with too much water. My blood ran down my finger with the animal's blood in a steady stream. Like two tributaries finding their way to the larger, more assuring river.

~

The time had come for Alia to go to Malir. I tried calling her on her land line again, but no one answered. Would I ever be able to talk to her again? I thought in exasperation. I watched movie after movie, read one book after the other, tried to occupy my mind.

Shahaan was the first to call me, to check up on me. "How have you been?"

"Just okay. Coasting."

"Have you heard from Alia?"

"No. Not anything."

I couldn't gather the energy to engage in conversation. I said something about my mother calling for me, and quickly got off the phone. I felt horrible about this, guilty. But my mind just wanted to be solitary. I will make up for this someday, I said to myself.

I often felt hungry in my room. I knew there were chocolate chip biscuits and salted cashew nuts in the kitchen cupboard next to the micro-wave in the kitchen. But I couldn't go there. He would be there. His glances seething into my skin and spreading.

And then there were the times when I couldn't help but wonder about Alia. What was she doing now? Was she feeling the same way I was—lost, unable to do anything? I started to remember this one girl in our ninth grade class. We were all told to write a poem on the subject of our choice and then read them out in front of the whole class. One girl, Sasha, had written a poem on life. A clichéd title. "Life is a Marathon Race," she said. "Each of us races forward, competing with others to reach to the end. We endure pain, sweat, and tears. But soon everyone reaches the finish line: death." The class fell silent for a while, and then broke out into snickers. Alia and I included. A boy had piped up, "Well I guess that means everyone wins the marathon!" We all laughed. We didn't want to face the reality of what she had said.

Why was I thinking about this now?

And then the day finally came. I checked my e-mail inbox and saw a message from Alia. My mind skipped with joy as I waited for the page to load. My excitement faltered when the page opened. The mail was brief. A mere four lines.

Hi, I have to make this quick—my mother will be back from my aunt's house soon. I've messed up—I've really messed up. I don't know what to do. I can't explain here. I can't believe what's happened, what's happening. Call me on the number written below at exactly 7:45. My mother will leave the house to go visit my Aunt. Don't call any sooner. Alia

I stared in consternation at the words. I couldn't understand what she meant. Had Alia been caught smoking? It could only have been that. But why couldn't she have just said so? I waited anxiously until 7:45.

Time inched along slower than ever before. At 7:40, I couldn't contain myself and rang her. The phone was ringing but no one answered. I tried again at 7:45. This time she answered.

"Hello?" her voice was uneasy, breathless. I had almost forgotten how she sounded.

"Alia?" My voice shuddered as well.

She let out a sigh and said, "Yeah, it's me. "My mother was just leaving when you called first, so I couldn't answer. H-how are you?"

Terrible. The last few weeks have been hell. "Fine," I answered. "But how are *you*? What happened?"

Alia's voice became muffled. She was speaking very, very low. There was probably somebody nearby. "I . . . oh, I don't know how to say this. So much has happened. I . . ." She sounded weak, tired.

"Alia," I said soothingly, "It's okay, calm down. Everything's okay—"

Alia smirked bitterly. "No, no, it is definitely not okay." The line was crackling slightly now. "You're going to hate me," her tone had dropped into a soft wail. "You are really going to hate me . . . I . . ." There was a bigger crackle this time. The line went dead.

I called again. And again. There was no tone. I frantically redialed the number automatically. After the twentieth time, I gave up. How would I reach her now?

It had never been this way with me and Alia before. She seemed so far now, so out of reach. I e-mailed her and then shut my computer. I tried to read a book but couldn't concentrate. I just had to know what had happened. There was a chance, I thought to myself, that Alia had called Shahaan too. Maybe she had told him something. It seemed highly unlikely that she would have rung him before me, but what had I to lose?

I rang Shahaan at a quarter to twelve. He answered immediately. "Wow," he said when he picked up. "Is it my birthday? I don't think I've ever been this spoiled."

I chuckled obediently. I then asked him if Alia had gotten in touch with him.

His tone changed and became graver once I mentioned her name. "Oh, so she told you."

My mind throbbed with angst. Alia had told him before *me*? I put aside my hurt for the time being and said, "No, she was about to tell me, but the phone went dead. Will someone tell me what's going on, for God's sake?"

Shahaan paused to consider and then said, "I really don't know if I should. I don't know the whole story, anyway."

"Just tell me what you know," I said impatiently. Another pause.

"I hate having to relay information between you two like this. Okay, I'll tell you. But you have to keep calm." He sighed. "A few days ago, I received a call from Alia. This was two days before she was leaving for Malir. She sounded really upset. I felt like she was trying to act normal but she just didn't sound like herself." He paused. "She asked me for some hash." He breathed.

"Is that all?"

"No. Okay. Please don't freak at what I'm about to say next. She wanted more."

"What exactly did she want?"

"Opium."

"Is this a joke? You have opium? How? And how does she know?"

"She knew because I guess her cousin, my buddy, told her I had some. I have a friend who gave some to me at a party. I never tried it. Just kept some with me because—I don't know—I felt like it might be valuable. Who knows how much it costs? I don't know. But basically, I said no to Alia, right? No way am I going to give someone opium when they've never even tried drugs before. Just a bad idea. So I said no.

"But she got on my case. Like really got on my case. She kept saying, 'This is the one thing I'm ever going to ask of you, Shahaan.' I told her she needed to calm down, take a few breaths, just relax. Eventually, she got calm, we talked for a couple minutes, and hung up. I didn't hear from her for a while. A few days go by and then she calls me out of the blue, and says, 'Can we meet? I just need someone to talk to.' I hear her crying on the phone. So I thought to myself, okay, my friend needs me there. I drove to her house and picked her up. She tells me she wants to go to a convenience store. She asks me if I will buy her some cigarettes, while she waits in the car. So I went. I got her a cigarette pack. I left the car for maybe five minutes.

"When I come back, I hand her the cigarettes. She suddenly says she wants to go home. It was weird. I said are you sure you don't want to talk about what's happening? And then she finally opened up. First she said she had just recently found out she got accepted into college in America. New York University. And that she was scared. Because she didn't think her parents would let her go. Something about her mother wanting to arrange her marriage with someone."

"Wait, what? Arrange her marriage?"

"Yeah. I just didn't get it. But she wouldn't elaborate. She just said her mother introduced her to some guy. And her family wants her to marry him. When she said no, her family flipped on her and now she's confined to the house. Can't go anywhere."

"This is not happening." I closed my eyes and sat down, defeated.

"Yeah, but that's not the end of it," Shahaan said. He cleared his throat. "I dropped her home, and on the way back to my house, I opened the cigarette compartment to my car. You know, where you guys saw some hash once?"

"Yeah," I said.

"All my hash was gone. Along with some other stuff."

"What other stuff?"

Shahaan paused. "The opium. I had only gone to the party a few days before, so it was still in my car. It's gone now."

"Are you kidding me?" I didn't know what to say. There were no words to say.

Silence stood between us stealthily. Finally Shahaan said, "The point is, Ayla, the only person who could have taken everything was

Alia. And she stopped returning my calls. I'd have gone to her house again but her parents will kill her if they see me."

"Why are you telling me this *now*?" I tried to keep my voice calm.

"I wasn't sure when, and how, to tell you. I thought if there was some way I could get them back without you knowing, it would be better for all of us."

"That was dumb."

Shahaan didn't reply. "I got an e-mail from her today."

"What did it say?"

"You sure you want to know?"

"Yes!"

"Okay. Just . . . just listen first. She said she was sorry she stole everything from me. And that she seriously regretted it. Because apparently the same night, she locked herself up in her bathroom, and smoked the hash and opium sitting on the side of her bathtub. Together. Her mother banged away on her door, and when no one answered, she got worried, and opened Alia's door with her spare keys. She found Alia lying dazed on the bathroom floor. At first she thought Alia had slit her wrists. But then she saw a cigarette filter in her hand and some tobacco lying on the tiles."

I almost forgot that it was Alia who Shahaan was talking about. As he went on and on, it seemed all the more unreal to me. Had things really come to this—where Shahaan had to convey to me that my best friend had tried drugs and had almost become unconscious? The agony of not knowing anything myself, of being so *distant*, numbed me.

"Are you there?" Shahaan asked.

"Mmm hmmm," I said.

"Are you okay?" His voice was soft, concerned.

I didn't know. I remembered the first time Alia and I had tried cigarettes, on a very hot, moist day in sixth grade. We had stolen some from Alia's father's study and hidden in her basement, giggling. The cigarette felt quite big in my small hand. It may have even been as big as my hand. Alia had twirled it between her fingers, remarking how it looked like a yan yan stick. We had filled our pockets with butterscotch sweets, in case the taste of the cigarettes was bitter. "It has no taste, silly," Alia kept telling me. But I stacked up on candy anyway. We sat in her basement and I inhaled on the filter deeply, thinking that I wouldn't really feel anything unless I did.

Alia was right. It didn't taste like anything. It was just a hollow feeling, like you were swallowing emptiness. When I told Alia this, she puffed and said slowly, "You have just swallowed death. What does it taste like?" The smoke breezed out of her mouth as she laughed. A thick blanket of smoke hovered around us, encircling us, ready to feed on us. In the end, we emptied our sweets from our pockets and devoured them. Sweets were better than cigarettes any day, we had both decided.

I had so many questions that I wanted to ask Shahaan. But I wanted the answer from Alia. "Did she tell you when she was coming back?" I asked him. He replied no. All we could do now was wait. Wait for some news.

By the time Shahaan and I had finished speaking, it was a quarter to two in the morning. Surprisingly, I slept soundly. It was a dreamless sleep, not plagued with fearsome thoughts like I had expected. I had to go to yoga class the next day. I saw it as a welcome relief. The worst thing for me right now was to stay at home and spend my time worrying.

I reached Ghazal's house fifteen minutes early. I performed my positions more keenly, trying to make my body relax where my mind couldn't. I knew Tanzeela had arrived when I saw her reflection in the mirror in front of me. For the first time ever, she looked frayed. Her hair was open and uncombed, her eyes heavy with bags, and her laces were untied. After class, when we met at our usual place beside the speakers to sip water, I asked her what was wrong. "It's just so . . . complicated," she heaved. I waited for her to go on, but she didn't.

"So it doesn't look like we'll be going to the café today," I grinned and offered her water. She didn't smile back. She was looking away.

"You don't know what it's like, Ayla. If only you could understand. I can't blame you for not. The thing is, there are times when I feel really trapped."

There it was. What I had been waiting to hear for weeks now. "Tanzeela," I said softly. "I think we should talk."

She looked worried. "I wish we could, I really do. But . . ." she glanced at her watch as if it were a signal wringing out her death sentence. "I have to go," she said reluctantly.

"Why?" My question came out harsher than I had intended it to.

"I need to get home," she answered.

"Why do you need to get home? What's the urgency?" I needed her to tell me. I knew the answer, but I just had to hear her say it.

Tanzeela looked quickly around the room, her long eyelashes quivering wherever her eyes moved. Everyone else had moved out and we were now left alone in the room. "I can't come here anymore." She started rubbing her hands together in her lap, unable to meet my eyes.

"Tanzeela," I said again tenderly. "What is really happening? Is it . . . is everything okay at home?" I tried to look into her eyes but she had lowered them. I looked down to her lap, to her fumbling hands. That's when I saw it. There was a brownish bruise on her wrist, teeming like a large, hideous scar. Her hands trembled and then her lips followed. Slowly her whole body started convulsing and she bent over my lap, crying. I waited for her to release her pain, stroking her hair while she sobbed. Finally, I asked quietly, "Did he do this to you?"

Tanzeela stopped crying, her body steady now, and looked up at me dazedly. "Who?"

I looked at her, as if my gaze enough would convey the obvious. "Your husband, Amar." I felt like I was in some horrible game show; I was being asked questions without knowing for certain the answers.

She looked confused. "Why would you think that? Amar has been anything but harsh with me."

I felt a sick feeling at the base of my gut. She was defending him despite what he had done. Was it that or was she in denial? "So Amar has never raised his hand to you?" I asked. "You don't have to defend him. Or deny it if it's true. What he's done to you is horrible. I just knew something was wrong."

Tanzeela blinked at me as if I were mad. She remained speechless for a few seconds and then seemed to understand what I had said. "It's not Amar," she said, more firmly this time. "He has never raised his hand to me. It's his mother."

The room became stark silent, as if a gunshot had just sounded. "His mother has made life burning hell for me." Tanzeela wasn't crying anymore. Her voice was solid, and full of bitterness. And then, while I sat there like a suspended Greek statue, my expression unmoving, Tanzeela told me everything; how her mother-in-law had restrained her freedom since the day she had stepped in into her new house. When she had first entered, a new bride, Tanzeela said, Amar's mother had been particularly kind. She had told her over and over how happy she was to have Tanzeela around; she had never had a daughter. She had tried to make Tanzeela's stay extra comfortable, laughingly telling her not to worry about cooking and cleaning; that they had more than enough servants to take care of that.

Then the day came for the couple to leave for their honeymoon. Amar wanted a picture of Tanzeela and him together before they left for the airport. Shumaila Aunty told them not to hold hands or lean on each other while she took a photo of them in the front yard.

"This wasn't the first time she did this," Tanzeela said. "Every time we showed each other some sign of affection, she would visibly get angry at us, lowering her eyes and abruptly leaving the room when we so much as held hands. That's not even all. She would tell me to sleep in a different room when Amar had an early start at work the next morning. 'You'll distract him.' Tanzeela mimicked sourly. "I was a distraction for him through and through. She just couldn't bear to see us both together.

"One day the maid came and complained to me. Her brother had just died and she hadn't been given leave to attend his funeral. I went to my mother-in-law to try to convince her to let the maid go. But she spat out at me, 'Then why don't you clean the house and wash the clothes? You'd like to see what it is like without the maid? Then take on her work.' After that day she made me do the housework. I lied when I said I have to supervise the gardener and the cooks. Yes, there are many servants in the house; there are sweepers and there are cooks. But she made me pull out weeds from her garden and cook her breakfast nonetheless."

"But," I interrupted, unable to control myself, "Didn't you ever tell Amar?" Tanzeela said she had. Many times. Each time Amar would go talk to his mother, and each time she'd promise that she would be milder. And she always was when he was around. But as soon as he flew out of the city—as he did so very often—she resumed her habits. She gave Tanzeela grubbier tasks every day.

Then one day, an old friend of Tanzeela's from school called her, apologizing for missing her wedding. Her mother-in-law had picked up the other line accidentally and heard her speaking to a man. She erupted, going around the house ranting that Tanzeela was having an affair. "That's why she didn't like me coming here to Ghazal's class," Tanzeela said. "She didn't believe that I was really going for yoga. She thought I was meeting my old school friends behind Amar's back. I was only allowed to come when Amar put his foot down and said that his mother was being ridiculous. 'She will go wherever she pleases,' he told her, 'so long as she is in this house.' My mother-in-law relented, so long as I came home before dark. I felt like I was a child again, you know." Tanzeela shook her head in amazement, "I had never felt so babied before.

"Amar left for Turkey last week," Tanzeela said. For two weeks. Her mother-in-law had been looking forward to the opportunity, when she knew that there was no one to defend Tanzeela.

"She came into my room one night, and screamed names at me; calling me a whore, a prostitute, saying she knew I was having an affair. She went to the trove I kept inside my closet; the trove filled with the clothes and jewelry my parents had given me before the wedding, and emptied it on the floor. She snatched my jewelry; necklaces that my grandmother had passed down to me, and said I didn't deserve them because I was an infidel. I tried to stop her and then she slapped me."

I looked at Tanzeela's shuddering hand and asked, "But how did *this* happen?" Tanzeela's voice quivered more with every word. Shumaila Aunty had ripped her bridal clothes to pieces and set them on fire. "A mad surge had come over her. It was worse than anything I had ever seen her do before." Tanzeela had panicked and tried to put the fire out with the only thing that was in her hand—a book. The pages of the book caught fire; and burnt right in her hands.

I was jolted with the memory of that day in the laboratory, during the K1 experiment. We had both tried to put out fires, I thought, tried to fight against what was uncontrollable.

And then I thought of Tanzeela's mother-in-law, and imagined the time when she had just been Shumaila Aunty, my mother's friend. I remembered her warm, pleasant smile and how I had been taken away by the way her soft, silk sari fluttered against her feet as she had walked over towards me. I thought of how she boasted that her daughter-in-law had great cooking skills and that all she had to do was "step aside" and watch Tanzeela take over house duties. She looked so proud. Only to terrorize Tanzeela minutes after we had gone? It couldn't be the same person.

That girl lying lifeless in the dark over her bathtub couldn't be Alia. It wasn't true just because Shahaan and Tanzeela had fed me each of these stories . . . was it?

"So how did you manage to come today?" I asked Tanzeela.

"She locked me up in my room. But she left the keys in her room." Tanzeela was sobbing now. "I cried and cried in my room until one of the servants heard me. The same maid who I'd given leave to. She had a soft spot for me, I think. She let me out. I grabbed whatever I could and just left. No one knows where I am right now. "My mother in law won't be back till late at night. I just needed to get away after being locked up for so damn long. I can't go back there." Tanzeela hung her head in her two hands.

"You need to think about getting out of that house. Permanently," I wanted to hug her and soothe her out of her misery, but more than that, I wanted her to be free. "Have you told Amar what's happened?" I asked, holding her burnt hand in my own. Tanzeela hesitated and then slowly shook her head. "Why not?" I asked heatedly. "You can't give her the satisfaction and let her do this to you again and again!"

Tanzeela looked down and nodded. "I can't tell him because I'm scared." She raised her eyes and looked at me. "Have you ever done that? Have you ever kept a secret, even if it had worked against your interest, because you're afraid of what will happen after, of the effect it will have?"

She wasn't expecting me to say yes. Of course she didn't expect that I would ever be in a situation that she was in right now. It couldn't have happened to me. But did it? Maybe it was the reason I hadn't told my mother what had happened that day in the garden ten years back, why I still couldn't tell her the anguish I felt whenever Ishaq was around. *The fault, dear Brutus, is not in our stars, but in ourselves that we are underlings*, Caius Cassis had said on a stormy night. It seemed a perfect match, but of a different nature.

The fault, it seemed, was not in our handicaps, mine and Tanzeela's, but in us.

15

Alia returned from Malir after three days. I knew this because she e-mailed me once again, writing, *"I'll tell you everything when I come back tomorrow."* And tomorrow had come. I didn't reply to her telling her that I already knew everything. I didn't mind her repeating the entire story to me. Perhaps it would finally make it real to me. She called me on the day she arrived and asked if she could come over to my house to talk. I agreed.

She was to arrive at four o'clock. I went about trying to clean my room, to make the place look spotless. I asked the driver to fetch brownies and *nimco* salted snacks from the bakery nearby. When the food arrived, I arranged it using the small, delicate cutlery that we reserved for guests.

I had never taken so much trouble when Alia had arrived before. The idea seemed almost ludicrous, treating Alia like a *guest*. But I hadn't had anyone over at my house for weeks. I pitifully felt deprived of human contact, like one of those inmates at drug rehab centers who dressed up carefully on visiting day for loved ones that they had never bothered to take the trouble for before. Suddenly, I felt like I had to make an impression.

When Alia arrived at the doorstep, dressed head to toe in mourning white, I didn't quite know what to say. She looked no different. Her hair was of the same length, her features rigidly the same. I had almost expected her to look completely changed; with longer, lankier hair, frail limbs, chipped teeth, swollen lids and red eyes. *Like a drug addict?*

I offered myself for a timid hug, but Alia latched on to me instantaneously, like a magnet to metal and threw her arms around me. "I'm so glad to see you," I heard her say.

"Me too," I said automatically. I *had* missed her these past few weeks, I really had. But, it seemed to dawn on me; maybe I still did miss her.

I wanted to lead her to my room, not that I needed to—she already knew the way. But all of a sudden it seemed more appropriate to take her to the drawing room. I didn't know why I felt so; it wasn't as if I was *afraid* to be alone with Alia in my room. But I led her to the drawing room, like I had led Tanzeela and her mother-in-law the first day they had come to my house, and seated her.

"Do you want anything—a cold drink, coffee?" I sounded even alien to myself. Alia looked at me strangely and slowly shook her head. I ignored her and went into the kitchen to get her Pepsi and biscuits. When I came back, she was still looking at me strangely, as if she had just discovered that I was bald. She didn't say anything as I put the tray of sweets and biscuits in front of her. Before I had the chance to sit down next to her, she said matter-of-factly, "You know what's happened." She was looking ahead, past the food tray and plates, and her arms were folded.

"H-how did you know?" I knew exactly how but wondered if she had sensed it.

"Oh, come on," her tone was acerbic. "You're treating me like a stranger in your house. You're making excuses to run out of the room and get me 'sweets.' You don't want to be around me." Her voice gave way in her last sentence and became a pained murmur.

My throat swelled up momentarily; I felt like the guilty child whose hand had just been spotted in the cookie jar. "I'm sorry." There was a tremor in my voice. "I'm just hurt by this all." Alia looked at me quizzically. Hurt by what? Her expression read: how dare you be hurt at a time when I'm the one burning in agony, when I've just made it through hell and back?

"Why did you tell Shahaan and not me? Why did you do it at all, you silly fool, how could you?" The dam had burst. "You were clearly upset about something for the past few months; there's a reason you started smoking, and tried . . . drugs. What was wrong? What was pricking at you this whole time, something so deep and secret that you couldn't even tell me?" I tried to stop myself crying. I looked at Alia for answers but she just shook her head back and forth and stared through me as if I was air. To my great surprise, she started laughing. Disgustedly. I was in the nightmarish game show again and was the center of ridicule.

"You know, I am not surprised," she said, still shaking her head. "It's just like you to tell me, after I have been through the most difficult week of my life, how much *you've* been affected by my, by my wayward actions, how much it's *traumatized* you."

"Well, it's because I'm worried about you," I said. "I've been waiting here, worried sick for the past few days, dying to hear any word from you—"

"You, you, you, you!" Her eyes sparkled with anger. "You always have to be the leading lady of the show, don't you? Try asking me what it was like for me. Try hearing *me* out before ranting on about your misery. Why can't you do that?" Her angry voice now collapsed and she broke down in tears.

I had seen Alia cry many times before. She had cried on my shoulder when her first puppy died, sobbed in my hands when she failed her calculus test. But now she crumpled to the side of the couch, away from me, her head buried inside her own arms. She was alone. Not because she wanted to be, but because I had abandoned her. I had heartlessly reprimanded her for smoking without trying to find out what had *caused* her to turn to cigarettes in the first place. I was pushing her away now, when she only needed me to forget about how I was feeling and focus on her pain instead. But had I always known about her pain? When I had read her song in the garden, I knew something was wrong. Why had I ignored it? I thought to myself in alarm. What kind of a friend was I?

I leaned towards Alia and hugged her, something I should have done long ago but couldn't find the courage. She shivered in my arms, gasping after every sob.

"Alia," I said softly in her hair. "You were the handicapped girl, weren't you?"

Alia turned to me in confusion. "Wh-a-at?" she said in between snivels.

"The girl in your song. It was you." Alia didn't register what I was saying at first. She stared as if waiting for me to continue. Her lips were swollen and red, and her eyelashes were spiked with tears.

I told her what had happened on that rainy day; how I had read the song without ever mentioning it to her. At first she seemed baffled, but then a knowing look crept over her face, as she realized what I was talking about.

"So you read it . . ." Alia averted my gaze, unblinking. I nodded, and repeated my question.

"I don't know if I was the handicapped girl," Alia shrugged indifferently. "Maybe."

I wasn't going to let it go easily this time. These were questions that I should have asked her years back. I needed to be there for her now.

"You wrote that the girl's parents chopped her wrists off. Is that how you feel?" Alia looked bothered, and seemed unwilling to talk about it.

"I don't know. I just never thought about it." She looked away, sending me silent signals to stop.

"I want you to tell me exactly how you feel, Alia," I said pleadingly. "I know I was wrong for not asking you, but you knew that you could always tell me. So why didn't you?"

Alia was picking at the stitching of the border of the sofa. She was smiling sourly to herself and shaking her head. "I guess it doesn't matter now." She sniffed quickly.

There was silence. I could hear the scrape of the gate outside as the *chawkidaar*—our gatekeeper—shut it. The biscuits lay untouched on the table in front of us. The ice cubes in the glass of Pepsi had now melted into tiny beads and were floating at the top of the drink, like little rafts on sea. It was silent enough for me to hear the minute hand on my wrist watch tick, hear the sound of Alia inhaling and exhaling softly. "I'm going to run away," she said. "So that no one forces me into this marriage."

The room was still silent. My heart pounded loudly and fiercely. Ayla finally turned to me. "When I told my mother I got mugged, do you know the first thing that she asked me?" I remained unmoving. "She asked me who I was *with*." Alia's eyes had become hollow, empty of any emotion. "She thought—still thinks that I'm having a relationship with Shahaan. No matter how much I deny it. And she figured that you had introduced me to him. That's why she stopped me from seeing you,"

Alia's entire neck tensed as she sniffed. "I just couldn't deal with things any more. My own mother treating me like dirt right after we had been held at gunpoint and refusing to believe my story . . . having no one to talk to . . . being wrongly accused over and over. I couldn't live with my thoughts. I just needed to feel . . . out of myself. That's why I did it."

She let out a sigh and closed her eyes. "Then I found out I got into NYU. I was so happy. I couldn't believe it. I got a full ride—a one hundred percent scholarship. You know that I was born in the U.S. before my parents moved back to Karachi. I was a year old. I've always dreamed of going to New York but have never been. And I'm a U.S. citizen, technically! When I got that acceptance letter, I felt like this was the message I needed from the world. I am meant to go to college. I want to study design. This is my dream. But my parents won't let it be."

"Have you told your parents you got in?"

"No. I meant to. I had my acceptance letter in my hand and was on the way to my mother's room to tell her. God, the first thing I wanted to do was tell my mom. She knows how much I've wanted this. Then I overheard her talking to my aunt when I was outside her room. She was talking about me. Saying I have gotten into the wrong company, that I'm out of control. They want me to get married to this boy who lives in London. He's an architect. If I tell my mom I got into NYU there is no way she is going to let me go."

"But your mom seems okay with you getting married and moving to London," I said. "Your family won't even let you leave the house unsupervised, but don't mind you moving all the way to London?"

"Believe it or not. I think my mother thinks as long as I have a ring on my finger and a husband to 'control' me I could move to the moon for all she cares." She turned to me. "I've never been to London before. I've only read about the city in books. Sherlock Holmes. I wrote an essay about that book in a class and fricking failed it. That's how much I know about England, or Sherlock Holmes. Or both."

"So you're going to run away?" I asked quietly, looking into her solid eyes. "Where will you go?"

"With you. To America. To NYU."

"What are you talking about?"

"I know you've been accepted to Cornell. Congratulations, by the way."

"Huh? No, you've got it wrong. I applied early decision. Haven't heard back yet."

"Oh no, you have," Alia quipped contentedly. "There's a fat, heavy envelope sitting by your gatekeeper's room addressed from Cornell University. I saw it on my way in to your house. Surprised he hasn't given it to you. But we know what the heavy envelope means. So congrats."

My mind was racing. I was holding my head now.

I got into college. I got into *college*. *Am I going to America?*

"It's quite simple." Alia was talking now but I could barely register her because my mind was switching in and out of joy, exacerbation, fright, jubilation. "You're going to Cornell. I'm going to NYU. The only difference is, my parents can't know about it. Now my Dad is smart and he's pretty good about tracing me in Karachi. But no way on God's planet is he ever going to expect that I'd run away to New York."

"Alia, what are you saying?" I asked.

"Look, I've thought about this for a while and it can work." Alia was speaking calmly now, even *reasonably*. "The engagement ceremony is in the summer. I will go through with it. By the time it's over, you will be ready to leave for college. I'm going to buy a one-way ticket to New York. We will meet at the airport and fly out together. No one will ever know where I've gone.

"I know what you're thinking," Alia said before I could interject. "What am I going to do when my parents send the police out to find me? When they think I'm dead? Look, I don't mind telling them where I am when I'm already in New York. I don't want them to think I'm hurt or in danger. By that time, I'm already away. They can't force me to come back. But if they know that I'm planning to go to college right now, they *will* make sure I don't go." Alia paused and then looked at me. "Are you with me?"

I held Alia by the shoulders. "Alia, listen to me. This is nuts." I pleaded, "You just need to talk to your mother. You need to tell her you got into college and that you a are not going to get married to—"

"Just please tell me you're with me. Because I can run away but I don't have the guts to run away to another country *all alone*. I need you there."

"Why can't you just convince your mother—"

"Doesn't it makes sense to you by now, Ayla? My mother is beyond convincing!" Alia rasped. She looked out of the large window behind the sofa. The sun was setting now, casting orange hues on Alia's face, setting the room aglow. It was a perfect painting for the few seconds that it lasted.

"I guess I got my answer." Alisa sniffed and then got up, saying, "I have to be home now." I leapt up and grabbed her by the arm, willing her to stay longer. She slowly raised her gaze to mine, and her stiff face now seemed to look pained. "I'm sorry for the hurt I've caused you." Her expression was genuine. A look passed between us that I couldn't really describe. It wasn't a look of anger or love. It was acknowledgement; of each other's faults, of how we regretted hurting one another when we didn't mean to.

As each moment passes by, the last moment is reduced to a mere memory. As Alia turned and left, I wondered fearfully if that was what was what had just happened; that the moment had lapsed forever. I didn't want Alia to be a memory.

~

I had to concentrate on my painting. It was taking far too long to complete. I had kept everyone waiting, denying them any hints or clues. What worth was it if I never managed to complete what I had set out to do?

I fished out my red and gold watercolors. I had started off with a clear vision—a portrait, a close-up on the face. But when I looked at my work now, my vision faltered, like a rickety door on weak hinges.

It had been a portrait of a bride. A young one. Someone that I knew. I had drawn in the gold-sequined red *dupatta* to frame her face; painted in her slender neck and shoulders. The only thing that was missing was the face. Tanzeela's face. It was certainly easier when you had the subject sitting in front of you, posing. It was even helpful if you had a picture. I was familiar with the arches and crests of her cheekbones, the angular degree at which her jawbone progressed towards her ear, the supple roundness and the upturn of those lips. The human face was indeed a landscape—of summits, peaks, and lakes of tears.

I had wanted to begin on Tanzeela's face. But when I looked at the near-complete drawing now, something had changed. Tanzeela was no longer a trapped bride, like I had thought, but a trapped daughter-in-law. *But that didn't change her face.* No, but it certainly changed my perception.

I prodded the paper with my HB pencil, sketching in a face that I perhaps knew better than my own. Nutmeg-brown eyes, slight, sloping scar next to the left ear from childhood accident. Triangular jaw, deep-set eyes. No, the two brow bones weren't symmetrical enough. I rubbed out the pencil lines and re-drew. Thirty minutes later it was done. Alia was the face of the bride. I needed to draw it to envision it; somehow, the picture in my mind wasn't enough. Once I had sketched in the features, I dabbed my paintbrush in the cup of water and added color to her face. Strokes of blue to emphasize the cheekbones, brown around the lids to bring out the deepness of the eyes. And it was done. A mirror image of her. Even I was surprised at the accuracy. My painting was finally complete, but I loathed it. I couldn't bear to look at what I had done, as if the image that I had created would come true now that I had drawn it.

If *I* couldn't stand to see Alia like this, how could Alia?

~

I went to the neighborhood park the next day. Shahaan was to come and meet me there by noon. We had agreed on the park because it seemed like the safest place to meet—quiet, peaceful, unsuspecting. We had no one to hide from, but every time we met now seemed like a crime.

The park was a large one. The grass was patchy in some areas and yellow in others. Walkers walked and joggers whizzed by. Polished benches gleamed in the afternoon sun, already dirtied with polka-dots of crow-dung.

Shahaan was there before me. He was sitting on a bench underneath a sprawling, ancient tree, with a leather pouch strapped over his shoulder, and a book in his hand. His face lit up when he saw me. I sat down beside him.

"How are you?" he asked.

"I spoke to Alia. Her parents really do want her to get married."

Shahaan shook his head and looked down. "She's only seventeen," he murmured.

"It doesn't matter to her family. The earlier the better, they would think," I said.

Shahaan nodded slowly. Silence ensued once more. It was always so easy to talk to Shahaan. There had never been a limit to our flowing conversations. What had *happened*? I looked at the strap-bag that he had bought with him, lying on the bench. "What's in that?" I asked, determined to make conversation.

"Oh, just some pictures I took" he said offhandedly.

"Of what?" I asked, interested. "Gardens, rivers, creatures?"

Shahaan shook his head, looking disgruntled. "You know there's more to life than pretty gardens and flowers. If you weren't so enclosed in your own life, you would notice."

"What do you mean by that?" I asked, taken aback.

"I mean, you're spoiled rotten, in case you haven't noticed. All you have to worry about is your next manicure at the spa and what time the tea party will end. Do you have any idea what's happening around you?" His voice was heated, resentful.

I didn't say anything. Instead, I picked up his shoulder bag and opened it. I flipped out the first large snapshot and looked at it. It was a picture of a young girl with dirty, matted hair and a razed cheek. She was on her hands and knees in a heap of garbage, looking for food. You could see the flies encompassing her cheek, eating away at her wound.

"You don't know what it's like to suffer," Shahaan's voice echoed behind me. I flipped to the next snapshot; this time a crippled man bent over, with two stubs on his wrists for hands, and decaying flesh on his chest. He was burnt head to toe. Lying not in a hospital bed in the intensive care unit, but stumbling along the streets. Begging.

"I didn't have to go far to find them," I could hear Shahaan saying. His voice seemed so distant. "Just down the street. And they're there on every street, at each traffic signal. You're so used to seeing them every day, decapitated and starving, that you don't hear when they tap on your windows, that you feel relieved when your drivers shoo them away."

I felt the sensation from my hands and feet escape, until I could feel them no more. I wanted to defend myself, tell Shahaan that I knew a lot more than he thought I did. But I had no fight left in me. I wanted to be there for Alia, focus on her grief instead of mine. I wanted to numb my own pain so that I could feel hers. But it was like trying to put a bandage on a fresh, deep wound; it didn't stop the blood from flowing.

I had had nightmares for days now. They were all the same; I was young, barely seven, chasing a large beach ball. I was running towards it, trying to catch it, but then I found myself running away from someone. I was being chased. My legs gave way beneath me and I fell to the floor, scraping my knee, as I was closed in on. Trapped.

Shahaan sensed that I was perplexed and turned to me. He shook his head in remorse. "I'm sorry, I didn't mean to be so . . . I don't know what came over me." He pressed his forehead and closed his eyes. "I've just been in a really horrible mood the whole day—"

I didn't even hear him. "My mother hired a new cook a few months back," I said. My voice was trembling like a withered leaf in the wind. I had to grip the seat of the bench firmly to stop my hands shaking. "He . . . he looks at me strangely." I knew I wasn't making sense, neither to him or myself. But Shahaan seemed to understand immediately.

"Oh God, he's one of those perverted bastards. Why haven't you kicked him out?"

My throat was swelling up; I was getting that same suffocating feeling I got every time Ishaq was in the room; as if all the doors were locked and there was nowhere to escape.

"It's bringing back all these memories." The whole park around me heaved and swayed. "When I was small . . . i-it's like it's happening all over again." I couldn't let out anymore. Shahaan seemed to sense that

I was going to cry; he placed his hand on my back and tried to soothe me as I fell on my lap, heaving with tears.

"Who did it?" Shahaan asked. I was gasping into my hands, my tears seeping in between my fingers. I had tried to forget it but it was clear as ever in my mind. I was six and a half years old. I couldn't remember my ninth birthday party, or my horse riding accident at ten. But I remembered this—vividly.

My mother had bought me a brand new beach ball on her return from France. It was a large, blue and red one; almost half my size. I had taken it to our front lawn to play with my puppy, Pesky. I had thrown my ball around the garden and watched gleefully as Pesky tried to catch it, tripping over himself. But the third time, I had thrown my ball too far. It had rolled off out of the garden, into the pond. Pesky tried to run after it, but stopped before the pond and whimpered helplessly.

I watched the beach ball bob up and down in the water. I wanted to save it before the water worms that lurked inside the pond engulfed it. I tried to lean over the rocks to grab my beach ball. But I miscalculated and tripped over the rock, plunging into the water. I heard faint sounds as I flailed my arms underwater: Pesky barking wildly; the birds chirping in singsong. And then there was that sound of droning hollowness that everyone hears underwater. As if the world has escaped from you. It was the only thing I could do; listen for sounds. I didn't know how to swim.

I couldn't remember exactly when I regained consciousness. When I woke up, I found myself lying flat on the grass, soaked from head to toe. I opened my eyes and saw Rahim, the cleaner, staring down at me, wondering if I was dead. He was trying to revive me. "Are you awake, *choti mehm sahib*?—little madam?" He asked in Urdu. I didn't know if I was. I could taste salt in my mouth, and my stomach hurt. But I couldn't open my eyes.

"Don't worry, you are fine," he assured. "I even took out your ball." I squinted open my eyes and saw him hold my beach ball, dripping with water. I shut my eyes again. Everything was quiet. I could feel grasshoppers inching their way towards me. And then I felt something else; something cold. His hand on my leg. It was clamped around my ankle, like a tight chain. His fingers slowly led their way up my leg. I was barely conscious; my brain was numb but my senses weren't. I could feel everything but was unable to stop it.

"You're all right, don't worry," he assured again, soothingly. I didn't believe him. If I was alright why was I feeling this way? Where was Pesky? I shivered in my wet clothes, as the wind hit me fiercely. He was stroking my arm now, and then my hand. I felt him take my own hand into his. What was he doing? This was a strange sort of game. I didn't want to be controlled like this; I wanted my own hand back. I pulled, resisted, but I wasn't strong enough. His grip was firm on my wrist. "It's okay, you're fine," he repeated, whispering now. He held my hand tight and placed it on his groin. My heart shuddered at the sudden, unfamiliar hardness. I wanted to be with my mother, lying curled up in front of the TV and watching Sesame Street like we did every Sunday. I could hear Pesky now; he was barking in the distance. Wildly and uncontrollably. A helpless witness. Like me.

"Why didn't you tell your mother?" Shahaan's voice loomed some-where in the background, like the sudden sound of a voice in the dark. I could tell he was trying to hold in his anger. My mother had been away in India at the time. How could I tell her when she had come back? There was no way I could describe what had happened. But even if there was, I was scared. Rahim had told me, after he had put my soaking shirt back on, wagging his finger in my face and crooning, "Now don't tell your mother, *choti mehm sahib*. She will get very angry with you if she finds out." His voice was still low and menacing, but soft. But how could I do that? I thought. I told my mother everything; what I learnt in school each day, which friends I made in class, and what kind of animals I saw in the story books. But I didn't want her to be angry with me.

"Ishaq has the same voice as him," I said, more to myself than to Shahaan. "That same low, luring tone. I can't stand being in the same room with him because it brings all those images back. I can . . . *feel* it happening again, to me."

Shahaan held my arm, firmly now. "Ayla," he said. "People like this deserve to be in jail. No, they ought to be shot. They don't deserve to be working in houses, with young girls around. And I know that now, after all these years, you don't think your mother will be angry with you."

I shook my head and squinted my eyes shut. "I can't, I can't, I can't. It's too late."

"No, it's not!" Shahaan looked as if he was ready to get to his feet. "If she doesn't kick him out, I'll fix that son of a bitch myself."

"No," I was adamant. "You're not getting involved. This isn't even important right now. Alia is being forced into marriage! We have to try to help her." A queasy feeling was emerging at the pit of my stomach. It had sown its seed the minute Alia had told me what had happened, and was now spreading its roots and blooming. I had tried to quell it for days now. Tried to ignore it. But I couldn't cover up my sins when they were so glaring.

"It's all my fault," I said slowly. "This would have never happened to her if it weren't for me."

Shahaan looked at me, bemused. "What, did you put the cigarette in her mouth?"

"If I hadn't convinced her to come to the exhibition, this wouldn't have happened."

"But how do you know she wouldn't have turned to drugs anyway?" Shahaan asked. "It's pointless to do that, it really is. Trying to retrace your steps, wishing you had done it differently. Don't do it. Whatever happened had to happen."

"I'm not a fatalist," I riposted. "I don't believe that it was God's will. It wasn't fate."

"That's interesting," Shahaan grinned. "The preacher of Islam renounces fate. You've adopted the Buddhist view when it comes to destiny then: nothing is determined."

"What are you trying to imply?"

"Oh nothing, nothing at all." Shahaan was serious. "I really don't have any problem with it, picking the best from every religion. You're not the only one to do it. In fact, you may not know this, but there are over six billion religions in the world."

"What?" I looked at him in disbelief. "That's outrageous."

"No, and it's rather obvious. I'll put two Muslims together; they both have the same major beliefs, in Allah, in the Holy Prophet. But one doesn't regard it important to pay Zakat. The other doesn't believe in killing goats. Their religion is the same, and yet different to each of them. Your religion is really your own. None of us in this world shares the same one." I wasn't sure what to say. My mind was registering what he was saying. But there was another part of me, wondering back to the day at the beach, when I had first met Shahaan. If I had never spoken to him, if I had just taken my paints and found another spot without bothering him, what would things be like? What would have happened if I had chosen a different cell phone shop to fix my phone, and never found him again? There would be no Shahaan. No exhibition . . . No marriage.

I had done this to Alia. It had all traced back to one simple action of mine. Not letting a stranger be just that: a stranger.

16

That day I met Shahaan in the park, I went home and prayed. I prayed earnestly, on my hands and knees, for Alia's future, for Tanzeela and her safety, and then, as an afterthought, for myself. I hadn't taken out the velvet prayer mat from my closet for over a year now. It was supple and soft from under-use. Maybe Shahaan was right. You were quickest to turn to God when you were in misery, and even quicker to turn away from Him when success befell you. But I needed to turn to God now. Shahaan's lack of direction where it came to faith had somehow pushed me towards my own.

Allah-ho-Akbar. God is great. I submitted myself in prostration, murmuring the Arabic verses under my breath. The call to prayer sounded faintly from my window. I thought in painful guilt how many times I had ignored the call to prayer; not turning the volume of my music down when it resounded in the air, as if by drowning out the sound I could somehow delay my duty, put it off indefinitely. Then who was I to tell Shahaan proudly, "I know enough about my religion to practice it"? His words resounded in my head. *You take on a religion and then seek to understand it.* Who was I to judge him for doing it the other way round? In the end, he was no more of a disbeliever than I had been.

⌐

"She won't listen to me," I told Shahaan blankly. We were back in his car, outside a CD shop on Ghizri Road. Hordes of people walked to and fro outside, like intermittent flies. The sound of indiscriminate chatter reached us inside the car. "She won't try to convince her mother out of it. I can just tell she won't."

"And she's agreed to the marriage?" Shahaan asked.

"She hasn't resisted." I gulped, resisting the urge to tell him what I knew about her plans of escape.

Shahaan switched on the car and let down the hand brake. "Where are we going?" I asked. He put the car in gear and stomped the accelerator. "Out of here. Somewhere else." Passerbys tentatively moved out of the way as we sped past.

I told Shahaan of how I had started praying again. "That's great," he remarked, looking at me sideways. "You know, I used to pray when I was little. My mother hired a *maulvi sahib*—a religious instructor— to come and teach me how to read the Quran, and to pray. Of course I never knew what the Arabic words meant. And I didn't know the meaning of the verses I was reciting during my prayers. But whenever I reached the *dua*, the final prayer part, I prayed really earnestly, for ages on end, promising God I wouldn't watch Power Rangers for a whole week if he answered my wishes."

I laughed, turning to him. "What did you ask for?"

"A chance to see my father."

There was an abrupt pause. "Shahaan . . . I'm really sorry," I said. I tried to imagine what it must have felt, to know your father was alive and well, and yet not be able to see him. "This must be so hard for you."

Shahaan turned to me and shook his head. "No, not at all. That was *then*. I don't ever want to see that bastard."

I swallowed. "Why?"

Shahaan was gripping the wheel rather tightly now. "Because of what he did to my mother. He made her promises, and then just said 'to hell with it' when they got married." Shahaan flung his hand in the air. "She left everything for him: her family, her job. And what did he do? He went right back to where he had started—in the mud." I had never heard Shahaan angry. I realized all of a sudden that I had never really asked him, probed him, to tell me what he felt about his parents.

We had pulled up outside a single-floor, decaying building, in the middle of a large garden. I looked around for a street sign, some indication of where we were. But it was completely pitch dark. I could faintly distinguish the dark silhouettes of the trees against the smoky fog.

"Where are we?" I finally managed to ask.

Shahaan got out of the car and opened my door for me. "You look so scared!" he laughed at my bewildered expression. "This is the place where I process my photos. No dead bodies in here." He grinned and turned around.

I followed him inside the building. There were no windows; it was a plain, rectangular block, one story tall, with a door. There was a large garden surrounding the building, with a narrow pathway in the center leading to the front door.

We entered a small room tinged with red. It was like viewing the inside of a room with red cellophane paper before my eyes. Everything gleamed scarlet. I blinked twice. There were long tables around me, and various types of paper stacked in one corner. And then pinned up against the wall were photographs: large ones, tiny ones, photos of wedded couples and of ladybugs and children.

Shahaan placed his bag on the floor and picked up a large, glossy sheet of paper. "I won't take long," he said.

I wandered around the room while he got about his business. "I've always seen these darkrooms in movies before," I called out to him. "Just never been in one." Shahaan grinned as he removed the film reel from his camera. "It's really not as glamorous as they make it out to be."

Shahaan had his back turned and was busy flipping through papers to find one of the correct size. I wandered around, looking at the photos pinned on the wall, trying to find a story behind them, feeling like a tourist in a historical building, marveling at the craftwork and wondering at the unfamiliarity. I sniffed and felt the potent smell of chemical in the room.

When I had tired of staring at the photos, I walked over towards Shahaan to see what he was up to. On my way, I spotted a low table that ran across half of the room, something like the work tables we had in the science labs. There was what looked like a rectangular basin, filled with liquid—chemicals, I presumed. Yes, I had seen those people in movies soaking pictures inside that liquid. I went closer to it, curious. And then stopped. There was already a picture floating in the eerie chemical. A sideways shot of a girl painting on a large sheet of paper on the sand, with the sunset looming in the background.

Me.

"W-when did you take this?" I asked dumbly. Of course I knew when he had taken it. The day was as clear in my mind as it was down in the glossy picture. Shahaan turned around distractedly and walked over. "Oh," he said, looking at the photo with me. But he didn't sound guilty, or nervous. "I was meaning to show this one to you one day. I think that's my best piece of work."

My eyes flickered slightly until I saw a stack of other photographs, lying to the side of the potent chemical. I picked them up and looked at each one after the other, my expression set like stone. There was a photo of me with my chin resting on my hand, lost. Another of me stepping outside a café, with the rain creeping through my hair. Me looking out the window, gazing at nothing at all. Another. And another.

"What is this?" I asked, not taking my eyes of the pictures. Shahaan laughed softly behind me. "It's funny you're so surprised. I'm no stalker. I don't think you realized, *still* don't think you realize, that I took all these photos right in front of you. Inches away from you." I shook my head and frowned. How was that possible? How could I be so absorbed in myself that I didn't even notice Shahaan snapping pictures of me, right in front of my face? I finally turned to him now, the photographs still in my hand. I looked at him for a minute, trying to find an answer on his face. "W-why?" I questioned slowly.

I had expected his face to reveal to me a map of answers but it emerged to me instead, a blank sheet of paper.

"Why?" he repeated, holding his arms out. "Is it really that unclear to you? Why did I put my life on hold so that I could meet you more, get to know you better? Why did I invite you and no one else, not even my own mother to the exhibition? Why did I chase you around town, trying to find where your yoga classes were so I could have some time to spend with you? Why am I only truly myself around you, and not Alia?" His voice was low, but heated. A soft flame from a glowing candle. He paused and looked at me. Not in hopeful expectation, but almost in empty sorrow. The look you gave the doctor right before he pierced the sharp needle through your skin.

I was unsure of what to do in a situation in like this. I wish I had the flair to react the same way Queen Elizabeth did when she was confronted with a suitor. "*Go, go, go, seek some otherwhere; importune me no more.*" Maybe I knew it all along. And then again, maybe I was unaware of it, as unaware as when he had snapped pictures of me all those times. But how did I feel? Within a second it was clear to me; I *did* feel the same way for him. Maybe I had felt it at the beach; when my heart was thudding out of fear, ignoring the voices in my head. Why else had I refused to turn away from him when I could have? Whether or not I was conscious of it before, it was unflinchingly obvious now.

My heart was beating again restlessly, prodding me to heed to it, to respond to its wishes. But the voice in my head grew louder this time, calling out lamentably, *if only it had been sooner.*

"I can't . . . can't do this." I found myself saying. Not now, when I needed to devote my attention to Alia, not when I was getting ready to go to college. I couldn't have a—the word suddenly seemed heavy, reeking of impossibility—*relationship* now.

Shahaan's face remained the same. He had been expecting it. Would he have never told me how he felt if I hadn't seen those pictures? Maybe not. He had looked as if he didn't want to tell me just yet; that he would keep it a silent secret indefinitely, or as long as it took till we reached the right time. But I had forced him to. My heart ached fiercely, almost punishing me for disregarding it. *Nonsense. There is no proof that the heart is directly responsible for emotions. It is only a pump. A sac of cardiac muscle and blood.* I knew that. But at this moment, only my heart could describe how I was feeling.

17

There was a popular saying that bad news often followed bad news. Not in my case this time. The next day I received a call from Tanzeela. I was surprised. She had never called me before. Frankly, I had thought that the stumbling day at yoga class was the last time that I would ever see her. I constantly thought about her after that day, wondering, *hoping* that she would find the courage to resist her mother-in-law.

"Hello?" she said, sounding unsure if she had dialed the correct number. When she was certain it was me, her voice relaxed. She sounded content, at peace. As she told me what had happened to her over the past week, I was convinced: yes, *good* news really could follow bad news!

Tanzeela's husband had returned from Turkey a week back. Tanzeela's hand had been healing, but the burn marks were still visible. Amar saw them and became visibly worried, prodding her to tell him what happened. She had said her hand had burnt while she was cooking. He didn't quite believe her. He asked the cooks and the maids in the house if Tanzeela's hand really had been burnt in the kitchen. All of them had been witness to the monstrous acts that his mother committed whenever he was away. But none were brave enough to defy their mistress.

They made up a vague story about how Tanzeela's hand had caught fire while she was making *puris*, deep fried bread.

Amar only saw what his mother was capable of when he witnessed her hit Tanzeela in front of him.

"She marched into my room one day and began tossing out clothes from my closet; trying to find evidence to prove my 'affair' with a school friend." Shumaila then came across some knee-length skirts and dresses—clothes that Amar himself had bought Tanzeela from his previous trip to Germany. Ripping them from their hangers, she marched to Amar in his room and threw them at his feet, saying, "Look! This is the only thing that slut is capable of doing—flaunting herself to other men in these revealing dresses while you're away!"

Before Amar could respond, Tanzeela entered the room. She saw her new clothes lying crumpled on the floor, and remembered how her bridal clothes had been snatched from her in the same manner, and ripped to shreds. She couldn't put up with this. Not again. She erupted. "Have you come to *this* out of your envy that your son has a wife?" she had demanded of her mother-in-law. As Amar looked on, flabbergasted, Shumaila grabbed Tanzeela by the hair, pulling at her fiercely.

"I couldn't keep anything to myself then," Tanzeela said to me quietly. "I pointed my finger at her, after Amar pulled us apart, and cried out how she had raised her hand at me time and time again, treated me like a slave, and how I had to battle with fire to save my own wedding clothes."

Amar had had enough. They could not stay in that house any longer.

"If that is what it took to make him realize what I was going through, I am glad that it happened," Tanzeela said solidly. "We are moving now. To a new house." I could sense the joy in her voice, the sense of release that she must have felt now that she was free.

I sighed and closed my eyes, smiling. "Tanzeela, you have no idea how happy I am to hear that." The nightmare was finally over for her. She had woken up to a bright day.

They were moving to a house in Phase Six; far, far away from Amar's mother's house in PECHS. Amar had ignored his mother's protests, vowing to her that he would have nothing to do with her ever again.

The new house was virtually empty. Tanzeela wanted to know if I would come with her to shop for kitchen accessories and bed sheets. I happily agreed; I wanted nothing more than to finally see Tanzeela untroubled, relaxed. This would be the first time. We agreed to go together the next day. As I put the phone down, I hoped to myself, wished deeply, that Alia would have the same happy ending.

Tanzeela picked me up the next day, in a chauffeured black car. She was wearing a lovely, deep blue *shalwaar kaameez*; very different from the dark clothes I had grown accustomed to seeing her in. I looked at her radiant face and thought: this is what any other nineteen-year-old girl would look like. Carefree, untroubled.

We went to the heart of Tariq Road to find what Tanzeela was looking for. Around us abounded the bustling crowd and the noisy traffic that were characteristic of Tariq Road. Also abundant were the rows of cramped shops, with their flamboyant shop names. *Just 4 You* clothing accessories was down the road from the *Fancy Lady* makeup shop. Neon, bright shop slogans glittered at us. The outrageous shop names were always a source of amusement to Alia and I, whenever we drove past Tariq Road. "*Fit Rite* shoes," Alia would chortle, pointing out of the window.

"Ah, that's good," I would say, laughing back. "But not as good as," and here I would point out of my window, "*Gaylord Drycleaners!*" We would bend over the car seat, erupting with laughter. I now looked out of Tanzeela's window, and the colorful shops seemed like blocks of stone; fossils reminding me of a time that seemed far, far behind.

We finally ended up at a kitchen utensils shop. Tanzeela looked around at the rows of the pots, pans and microwaves and said, her eyes widening, "I can't believe I'm really doing this. It all just seems so unreal." I smiled at her, saying that her married life had only now truly begun.

We looked around and tested some utensils, and bought two frying pans and a wok. We left the shop and went to another, bought some more things and moved to another. As we left from the fifth shop to walk over to the sixth, Tanzeela suddenly stopped. She was standing before a glass display, staring at a pair of silver shoes. I stopped next to her and looked at them. They were mounted on a smooth, silver heel, thin as a birthday candle. The front of the shoe was glass-like—translucent but sparkling against the light. They were what I really imagined Cinderella to wear.

"I want to try them on," Tanzeela said dazedly, hurrying into the store, hypnotized. The shop was very busy; women in their *chadors* and shawls tried to balance their screaming children while trying on their shoes. There were store clerks everywhere kneeling before women to help them put on their shoes; Prince Charmings helping hordes of Cinderellas try on their glass slippers.

Tanzeela managed to get a clerk to find the shoes and bring them to her. He came to her with a shoebox and set the sandals before her, offering to put them on.

"No, it's all right," Tanzeela insisted, and looked at me, saying, "I'm quite capable of putting on my own shoes!" The clerk looked at her from where he was kneeling and said, in crisp English, "Only trying to help, madam." We both looked at him in amazement. He had round, innocent eyes and was slightly overweight, balding from the head. His expression was positive, but not smug. Tanzeela blushed in embarrassment and tried the shoe on. And it truly was a Cinderella moment; they were the perfect fit.

As Tanzeela paid for the shoes at the counter, I couldn't help but gaze at the balding man who had brought the shoes to her. He was now totaling the bill and writing her a receipt. I could never recall whole faces, but I never forgot a feature. An indistinguishable jawbone, a sharp nose, a heart-shaped hairline. And there was something about this man's chin that seemed haltingly familiar. Square and then slightly round at the tip, like whipped cream at the top of a sundae. It was Shahaan's chin.

"Here you are," the man said to Tanzeela, handing her the bill. He must have noticed me staring at him. He looked at me and Shahaan's eyes bore into me. I stood before Shahaan's father, gazing as he carefully wrapped each of the sandals and placed them inside a white shoebox. I tried to look away and fidget with my purse. Tanzeela and he conversed for a few minutes, during which he revealed that he owned the shop. My mind went back to Shahaan's words, *he opened up a shop in Tariq Road.*

I stood there, head down, my head buzzing as Tanzeela paid the bill. Of course the man before me only saw me as a customer, and nothing else; not a link to the son that he didn't even know he had. The man asked Tanzeela, mid-sentence, nodding towards me, "And wouldn't your friend like a pair of shoes as well?" He smiled kindly, with Shahaan's twinkling eyes, looking at me. I shook my head and said no. And then Tanzeela and I left the store.

I didn't tell her anything. I didn't quite know how to say it. She noticed me looking a little dumbfounded, but I declined that anything was wrong.

Shahaan didn't know exactly where his father worked. Now I did. He had no idea how successful his father's shop had become. I would have to keep this nugget of information to myself, like I did everything else. Even when it tormented me. But maybe if I didn't, Shahaan would finally be granted the love of a father, and the father with the knowledge of Shahaan. Each of them would routinely carried out their lives now, unaware that the other existed.

I almost chuckled to myself thinking that if I did tell Shahaan anything, I would let him know, and proudly at that, that his father finally *did* learn English.

18

I came back home in the evening to find my mother crying. She was sitting in the lounge, head resting against the palm of her hand, sobbing quietly. I didn't think she had heard me come in. I put my bag down on the chair and faced her. "What's wrong, Ma?" She wouldn't look up at me. I went and sat down next to her. The sofa heaved slightly under the additional weight. "What happened?" My father was not in town; they couldn't have had a fight. Why? I thought to myself, why was everyone around me breaking down into tears, each with something in their heart broken? I felt like I couldn't take any more of this; the misery, the pain of others.

My mother sniffed abruptly and straightened up. She then turned to me, her face smoky with dripping mascara. "It's the cook. Ishaq." My heart cringed at the sound of his name. I remained silent, listening. "Ishaq and Asad had been playing cricket in the garage. After they had finished, Ishaq came up to him and . . ." My mother's voice drowned out into a moan. I couldn't urge her to go on . . . I could barely speak. My throat was hard and dry, as if I had just swallowed gravelly sand. "He took advantage of my boy," my mother wailed, covering her eyes.

"What did he do?" I finally found my voice. "Tell me, Ma, what did he do?" I didn't realize that I was shouting. "He's been doing it for months," my mother cried. "I only found out because I walked into the garage to find the garden hose." My mother closed her eyes; the image was too horrifying; for any mother to see. "I saw him with his pants down," she said quietly. "Grabbing Asad by the arm, *forcing* him to . . ." She shook her head, unable to continue. "He told Asad that he would break his neck if he told me. And it happened again and again. While I did nothing. I couldn't even protect my own son." She wailed and then burst out again. I stood there, still, hearing the echoes of my mother's cries throughout the house. The only sound that I could hear in that silence. Louder than the thoughts in my head.

"What did you do?" I asked. She paused amidst her sobs and looked at me strangely, surprised that I hadn't expressed any shock, any feeling. "I threw him out," she finally said. "There was nothing else I could do. Your father is not in the house, or he would have ripped him apart with his own hands."

That was it. He had gone. He was out of my life, finally. Kicked out graciously. As if he was a tenant that had refused to pay rent and not a man that had just molested my brother. He would roam about the streets for a few days and then find another job at another house. Where he would do it. Again. Just like Rahim.

"Mom," I said. "I was sexually molested by the cleaner when I was seven." I had said it without feeling, as if I were telling her what I had had for lunch the previous day. *No more secrets.* Tanzeela had revealed hers, and now it was my turn. Perhaps one day Alia would reveal hers, too.

I knew it was the worst time to bring up this piece of information. I didn't want to make my mother more upset. Only up until this moment, I had thought that she would be upset with me. For not resisting when I could have.

My mother stopped sniffing. She was looking down at the carpet, a faraway look on her face. I wondered if she had heard me.

"I know, Ayla," she said to me, a grave look on her face. "I found out as soon as I came back from India. The maid had seen everything. She was cleaning inside the house at the time. She saw what had happened from the window. Rahim had forced her to have sex with him before. He was a heroin addict. Your father almost killed him the day he found out; he beat him until his eyes rolled up in his head. Your father would have murdered him; I saw it in his eyes. But I stopped him. I didn't want us to be murderers. We sent him to jail immediately." I remained quiet for some time, trying to let her words register. "Why . . . why didn't you tell me?" I whispered, looking away. My mother reached out for my hand. "You were seven, Ayla. You had already suffered from the shock. I made sure never to leave the country again while you and you brother were at home."

I wanted to tell her more. That I still had dreams of Rahim chasing me, and me running as fast as my legs could take me, how I was never quick enough to escape his grasp. And all this time I thought he was still out there, lurking and ready to come back, and find me. My mother had known all along. It wasn't a secret. And she wasn't upset with me. Rahim had said she'd be angry at me enough times so that I truly thought that she would, even years later. I felt a tear gather and roll down my cheek. And then more followed, but they weren't tears of sadness. It was out of relief. My mother really wasn't upset with me, I closed my eyes and told myself. Rahim had been wrong. Thank God.

It really wasn't my fault.

~

I had framed and hung up my painting of Alia in my room. I had made her a happy bride; not beaming from ear to ear but content, a soft smile on her lips. She was on top of my dressing table now—sparkling, gorgeous. I was still waiting to hear word from her: this is what our relationship had deteriorated to; long moments of silence punctuated by brief spells of contact. The rest of the time was just spent waiting.

I received a call from Tanzeela again. She was giddy with excitement. She tried to contain herself but couldn't.

"I just took the test . . . I'm having a baby." There was a pause.

"What?" I shrieked into the phone.

She laughed. It was the happiest I had ever heard her. In the depth of my heart I knew this was just what she needed; a new start, a new family that she could call her own.

"That's fantastic," I said, congratulating her. I couldn't have hoped for better news at a time like this. Tanzeela then invited me over for dinner at her new house.

"There isn't much furniture and it's still mostly a mess," she said, laughing, "but we would love to have you over. Amar really wants to meet you as well. I tell him so much about you."

I was more than pleased to come, I said.

"But really," Tanzeela said. "I have never thanked you. You are the only one who I confided in at the time that everything happened. And who knows, I might have never found the strength to tell the truth if you hadn't insisted that I should." I told her not to think about it, thinking inside, *and I may have never found the strength to tell the truth if it weren't for your influence.* But everyone had secrets. No matter how much they revealed, or admitted in confidence. Everyone had untold truths, tucked away in a dark place, truths that would astonish others if they knew, truths that could get us into trouble. But we couldn't tell anyone. Not even those closest. Because after all, as the verse in Arabian Nights best put it, if you couldn't keep your own secret, how could you expect others to?

19

6 months later

"I hear Alia's fiancé grew up in London," my mother told me as she dabbed lipstick on her lips and pouted in the mirror. My mother pinned her ears with gold earrings and looked back from her reflection to me. "He doesn't speak a word of Urdu. A *pakka firangi*—a true foreigner. But such a smart boy. Lives in a town called Surrey and works in the city."

I didn't answer. My mother continued, "She'll have so much fun moving to a new city!"

The day of Alia's engagement ceremony was here. We had made it through the last six months of school, ambling through our final exams, thanking our teachers and hugging our friends goodbye: "*Add me on Facebook so we can keep in touch when you move to America!*"; "*Don't forget to send me pictures of your new friends, your new dorm, everything!*"; and "*You better come back to Karachi to visit—reunion in 2009!*" Somehow we had graduated, and Alia had still not bleeped a word to anyone about getting into NYU.

It was now July and barely a week before I would pack my things up for college. My visa was stamped onto my passport, my I-20 college verification issued. Everyone in my family was ecstatic and spoke about nothing else but my imminent venture to a new country. My mother had already given me a list of makeup items to buy from Nordstrom once I arrived in New York, so I could dutifully ship them back to her.

"It's hard to believe your friends are already getting married." My mother again turned back to her reflection in the mirror, adjusting the border of her sari. She was wearing a gold blouse with embroidered leaves and sequins. Her shining earrings twinkled in the mirror. "Alia is only eighteen years old, isn't she?"

"Yes, Ma. And she's only getting engaged. Not married." Images of Alia's tearing face emerged in my head. *I'll make it through the engagement ceremony.* "Technically she's not even engaged yet."

My mother looked back at me, delivering a look of wan pity. I stood behind her in a blue *ghagra choli*, a long embroidered pleated skirt with a stitched blue blouse. Together, my mother and I looked perfectly poised to celebrate, like honorary regal guests of the evening.

"I can see why you're your upset, *jaan*, love." My mother nodded in understanding. "Your childhood best friend is getting married. You're moving away to a different country and you don't know when you two will see each other again. You must feel so nostalgic. Of course it isn't easy seeing Alia married. Are you going to see her before you leave for America next week?"

"I don't know," I quickly looked away. In my mind, I knew what the answer was: no. Alia and I had spoken about our parting, many times over. She had somehow forgiven me for not agreeing to whisk her away to New York. "I guess we'll just say goodbye when you leave." She had told me at school on the last day of our final exams.

"Alia, please don't make me feel responsible," I told her. "If you are planning to do this on your own, go ahead and do it. But I can't be an accomplice in helping you run away. My family would never forgive me. Your family wouldn't. I would have helped in breaking your engagement and absconding from the country. I can't be the one to do that."

"I don't hold you responsible, Ayla," Alia had said. Her face was calm, even peaceful. "Maybe this is a sign that I am just not ready to go to college yet. Whatever happens, whether this wedding breaks off or not, you are not to blame. I dragged you into all of this. Your future is important. You go to America and begin your life and kick butt at college."

Because I can't. I almost heard the unspoken words in her silence.

"You know I won't be able to just enjoy myself as if nothing happened, Alia." I said, through gritted teeth.

"How about this, then? Just be there for me by coming to my engagement," Alia said. "Can you do that?" She smiled. "I need some support to get through the night—my God, I'll be fake smiling and chatting with a hundred people I'd rather never see again. Help me out there, okay?" She grinned and I tried to smile.

So here I was. Making my way to the engagement. This was the last time I would see Alia before leaving and I couldn't bear the thought. But I had something to give her. A parting present. I packed up the canvas in the car as my mother and I made our way in.

Twenty minutes later we were outside the engagement venue at the Sheraton Hotel. Contrary to what Alia had said, there were not one hundred, but *five* hundred people invited. My mother told me this in the car and I could see as much, because getting out from the car into the lobby, I saw scores of women dressed in wedding attire and carrying diamond clutch purses. Women who were now greeting my mom and touching my cheek and telling me how pretty I looked. "Your daughter is a true doll." A lady wearing a stupendously large pearl ring on her finger touched my arm and gleamed at my mother. "Our children grow up so fast, don't they?"

"Oh, they do," my mother smiled and chatted with the lady as I scanned the ballroom quickly, searching for a glimpse of Alia. "She's going away to college next week. And just yesterday I remember dropping her off to her first day of kindergarten. The time just flies by without a moment's notice!"

"Which college are you going to?" The woman's pearl ring, glaring and humongous on her dainty hand, was now making its way back to my arm, beckoning for attention.

"A college in New York." I said absent mindedly.

My mother clucked amusingly. "She's so modest, this one," my mother said. "Ayla got into an Ivy League school." She turned to me and laughed. "Tell Naila Aunty how you had the admission letter sitting at our house for weeks before we even realized it was there!"

The room suddenly became very quiet and we turned to the front entrance. I heard hushed whispers. "Look, it's the bride!" I turned and looked. Alia emerged in a flowing peach dress, her hair high and curled, diamonds sitting on her neck and forehead. She looked like the goddess bride I had envisioned. Poised. Airy. Gleaming.

Next to her stood a man who was tall. Her fiancé-to-be. It hurt me to admit this, but he was indeed really handsome; I was hoping he'd look menacing, a clear aberrant choice that would validate my disappointment with her family. A lean jaw and dark eyes framed his beaming and kind face. The two—Alia and he—were looking at each other, smiling. To the whole world, they must have looked like they were truly in love. Alia was making eye contact with guests and nodding, warmly hugging people and thanking them for coming. A natural hostess.

She finally made her way to me and my mother. I tried to get words out but found I couldn't even speak.

"Congratulations, Alia!" My mother spoke on my behalf and embraced Alia. "You look absolutely stunning, my child."

"Congratulations, Alia." I found the courage to smile and hug her as well. We then turned to her almost-fiancé.

"This is Saad," Alia said, turning to the tall man. He held out his hand. "Saad, this is—"

"Ayla," Saad interjected. He smiled and reached out to shake my hand. "Alia has told me *so* much about her painter friend. I see you are the only one holding a canvas in this room. So it had to be you. You really gave it away!" His accent was polished, unmistakably British.

"Here, let me introduce your mother to my mother. It really has been years since they've seen each other." Alia took my mother's hand and soon they were off, drifting into the center of the room, leaving me all alone with Saad.

"So you and Alia are childhood friends?" he asked. There was laughter and chatter all around us. He had to speak loudly for me to hear him over the music, and his deep voice boomed out musically, strong, and confident.

"Yes. We go back a long way. This is the first time I've seen her this dressed up for anything—I can hardly believe it's her!"

Saad laughed. "Alia's been running about greeting people the last few days and it's been insane for her, I'm sure," he said. "I'm hoping she'll feel more rested when we move to London."

"When is that going to be?"

"After the wedding. In a few months."

Saad's tone suddenly changed, "Listen Ayla," he scanned the room to make sure no one was listening. "I'm saying this to you because I know you're Alia's best friend. I know that she doesn't want this wedding to happen. I'm not an idiot."

My throat felt heavy. I gulped. "Why would you say that?"

"I know that she was caught sneaking out of the house to see some guy. Presumably a boyfriend."

"Shahaan?" I almost spit out the Pepsi I was drinking. "No, you've really got it wrong—"

"It's cool, okay?" he said discreetly. "I get it. She has a boyfriend. Whatever. I have a girlfriend in London. This is a purely arranged marriage." Saad laughed a little. He used air quotes for the word "arranged," and as he lifted his arms, I caught a glimpse of his silver Rolex watch. "Look, the point is, neither of us wants this. But this wedding is going to happen. We've spent fifteen thousand dollars on this engagement ceremony alone. Our parents get along. I'm willing to bring a 'good wife' back to London if it means my father will finally stop getting on my case about marriage and just let me live my life." A waiter now approached us with mini crab cakes and Saad dutifully plucked a crab-covered toothpick from the waiter's plate. "Thanks." He smiled widely at the waiter and swiftly put the crab cake into his mouth.

My ears were ringing and I looked across at Alia from where I was standing. She was taking photos with our friends from high school, laughing luminously and covering her mouth.

"D-does Alia know you feel this way?" I had to strongly resist my urge to empty my Diet Pepsi over this man's head, drown his precious designer navy suit.

"Yeah. We both know we don't want this. We've talked about it. The only difference is, I'm willing to go ahead with this wedding, but I sense she isn't. I can just see something lurking in that face of hers, I know she's scheming. But I'll tell you this. I really suggest you caution Alia that if she tries to avoid this wedding, and creates a scene, or runs away with her boyfriend, that she's really asking for trouble. It will be humiliating for the family. My father will never live it down. Alia's fate is decided. I think it's time she realized it."

And with that, Saad swiftly finished his last bite of crab cake, and airily walked away. He resumed shaking hands with men, uncles and aunties, nodding and leaning in and making jokes, dangling that British accent and Rolex watch in their faces till they were dazzled and overdid themselves with laughter at his charm.

I tried to make my way to Alia as fast as my feet could carry me, but it was too far. She was swamped in a mob of well-wishers. When I got close to the huddle around her, I heard an indistinct cough on a microphone and a glass being chimed.

"Please make your way to the stage, ladies and gentlemen." Alia's father was on the stage with a microphone and clearing his throat. He was sweating and looking visibly conscious of being on a stage in front of five hundred people. "The ceremony is about to begin."

I watched, dumb as a statue as Alia made her way to the elevated podium, a stage adorned with pink flowers and velvet chairs. Now Saad, too, was on the stage and procuring a ring case. There were flashes of cameras and phones being raised in the air in unison to capture the moment. Echoing applause as Saad placed a twinkling diamond ring on Alia's finger. I saw Alia's mother standing behind her, blinking away tears of happiness, clutching her chest and turning to Alia's father in delight. I had never seen her so overcome with emotion.

"A ring for my lady," Saad joked as he placed the ring on Alia's finger. My mother was now back next to me and whispered in my ear. "What a handsome guy. Those two are really made for each other."

I watched in mute silence as Alia then placed a ring on Saad's finger. He joked again, "I guess it's official now, ladies and gentlemen!" Everyone around the couple laughed. What a showman. The two then turned to the scores of photographers and smiled for the camera.

My feet suddenly found life and started moving toward the stage. Quickly and deliberately. My mother stared after me, confused as to why I had taken off. I literally jumped on to that stage, just as Alia was posing for a photo with her uncle and touched her arm.

"Alia," I was now aware of hundreds of eyes staring at me, wondering in consternation. I gently tugged at her arm. "Can you come with me for a second, please?"

"What's wrong?" She looked concerned, her kohl-rimmed eyes big with worry.

"Nothing. Um—I have something to give you." The canvas painting would just have to be an excuse. I felt Saad's eyes follow us, burning beams into our backs as we made our way out of the ballroom.

Alia's family—her aunts and uncles—gazed after at us for a second, and then resumed taking pictures. That's all you had to do distract someone: place a camera in front of him/her and a wobbling man with his thumbs up yelling, "Cheese!"

"Are you okay?" Alia asked, as we made our way outside the ballroom and into the lobby of the hotel. Waiters were busily walking by us with arms raised high, carrying trunks of steak, lamb, biryani, and dessert, ducking out of our way to avoid us.

I paused and just stared at Alia for a brief moment. A memory suddenly flashed in my mind, out of nowhere. I was nine years old and Alia had just turned ten. We were climbing up Alia's rockery—an outdoor tall rock decoration—outside her house. We didn't see the rockery as a piece of decoration; it was another child's playground, like every other place. Alia was in front of me, trying to grab on to the rocks to hoist herself up. "Don't grab the sharp rocks," she called out to me, behind her. I sheepishly looked down from where I was mounted. There were rocks everywhere, beneath us, below us. If I fell down I would plunge into those rocks, and roll down them like a small pebble. I turned back and tried to follow Alia, placing my hand on the soft rocks, and hoisting myself up. But my hand had gripped a loose rock; I tried to pull myself up and the rock fell out. I slipped and shrieked, thinking that I was sure to die.

But out of the dizzy blue, I felt a hand grab my own and hold onto me firmly, with a tight grip. Alia pulled me back up, smiling at my white face. "It's okay," she grinned, her brown eyes gleaming against the afternoon sun. "You're not going to fall while I'm around!"

"Alia, take this." I handed her the painting. "I want you to take this and place it somewhere. And then destroy it. You are not going to be a trapped bride. I can't watch it. This painting is a lie, okay?"

Alia released the canvas cover and held the painting out in front of her. The portrait of herself, in red dress, as a bride.

"Is this me?" she asked. "This is the secret painting you've been working on for months?" I couldn't let her continue.

"I am going to miss you," I said.

"Are you leaving already?" Alia said, her brown eyes glassy with hurt. "I won't see you after today, you know that? You're leaving next week."

"Yes, I'm leaving."

"Why are you saying bye to me now? Like this?"

"I need to say bye now. And I need to say again that I am going to miss you."

There was a pause. I took a deep breath and continued.

"Because NYU is four hours away from Cornell. And that's going to be a whole lot of driving to come out and see you." There were tears in my eyes and they were falling freely now.

Alia looked at me, silent. She saw my sad smile and held my hands in her own. We stood there for what seemed like hours, holding each other's hands, looking at each other as if to wish away the last year's happenings and all the dread and fear that had come with it. Alia's aunts were now making their way to her from the ballroom and calling out to us noisily. "Are you crazy leaving the ceremony like that? Everyone's waiting, *beti*—child! The food is already laid out!" The aunts busily took Alia's hand and led her away.

Alia couldn't help the smile that came over her face as she turned back to me, her deep eyes glowing mischievously underneath dark lashes.

The happiest bride-to-be ever.

Epilogue

"We've been through your luggage and you're all clear. You are free to go, miss." The blue-uniformed officer nodded at me primly and handed me a yellow card. "Please make your way over to baggage terminal A."

"Thank you." I took the yellow card from him, the document that marked my release, and made my way to the door entrance. The bearded Pakistani man who I had spoken to earlier was now gone. Only a smattering of people were left in the further investigation room, half of them nodding off to sleep.

It had been four hours since I made my way into the investigation room. I checked my phone and saw several *Whatsapp* messages. Three from Shahaan. *Have you arrived yet? What's the weather like? Take a picture of the statue of liberty—I'm waiting for it. Now.*

Outside in the baggage terminal, my bags waited. Two black lumps heaped on top of one another. The terminal was practically empty. Hollow. The only sound in the terminal was that of rotating carousels humming gently. I collected the bags, and turned to the only other figure in the terminal. She was sitting on a chair by the biggest carousel, a book in front of her, trying hard to keep awake.

When she saw me she jumped up. "That took a long time!" Alia exclaimed, hoisting her heavy backpack on her shoulders. Her hair was tied up in a ponytail. It was swinging freely side to side as she made her way to me.

I joined her and we both stared ahead at the sliding doors that led to New York. "Taxis this way," an arrow pointed.

I let out a big breath and turned to Alia. "It's time to do our first quintessential American thing," I said. "Hail a cab."

We walked in the direction of the sliding doors opening onto the pavement and the city beyond. Unbound. Untethered. Free to be. Waiting to live.